THE CHRISTMAS EVE WEDDING

C.S. Kjar

THE LAVENDER PEN

Available in eBook and Paperback

Paperback ISBN: 978-0-9985897-7-0

Digital ISBN: 978-0-9985897-6-3

https://cskjar.com

This book is dedicated to everyone who loves to read on snowy days. Sit back with a hot beverage, warm socks, and this book. Let the flakes fall where they may.

CHAPTER 1

‧‧٧‧٧‧٧‧

Snowflakes swirled and tapped on the window panes of Spruce Canyon Lodge, eerily asking to come inside. Frost along the edges of the glass gave a winter wonderland ambience to the banquet hall where a huge Christmas tree sat in the corner. Gifts circled the base of the tree, adding a bit of mystery and anticipation about what they might hold inside. It was Christmas Eve, a special and sacred time.

But for Ashley Chen, this Christmas Eve was dark and ugly. She sat staring out the window, the organza billows of her wedding dress piled around her like the snow drifts that were forming on the deck. Her long-planned wedding was in ruins. Buried under two feet of snow and a mound of betrayal.

The storm had partly spoiled her wedding. The worst blizzard in the last forty years hit the Colorado mountains last night. Wedding guests were stranded in Denver because of icy roads or at home because of cancelled flights. Both of her sisters had made it to Denver on the last flights in, but were stuck at their parents' house, unable to drive to the lodge. The groom's brother couldn't fly in from the East Coast.

Soft footsteps sounded behind her. If she ignored them, maybe the person would go away. She didn't want to see anyone. She didn't want to be pitied. She didn't want someone trying to make her feel better.

Her fingers caressed two beads on her bodice, fighting the urge to rip them off. Her wedding was off. Why shouldn't the beads be off too? Her anger might be assuaged if she gave them a mighty pull and flung them across the room. If she hit whoever was walking up behind her, the person might get the hint that she wanted to be alone. Her dark mood was about to force her into action.

"Ashley?"

The gentle voice of her uncle patted her bruised ego. Her favorite relative was the one exception to her rule. His wisdom was welcome any time, except now.

"Where is everyone?" he inquired. "We shouldn't let the weather postpone the wedding. Everyone necessary is here. Bride. Groom. Preacher." He let out a light cackle. "Let's get this show on the road!" He clapped his hands together and laughed.

Gritting her teeth lest she breathe fire on her favorite uncle, she kept staring out the window hoping to absorb some of the chill to calm her anger. He deserved an answer, but the words she would have to speak would make the nightmare real.

She looked up at her Uncle Don. Her clueless Uncle Don. He'd gone to the trouble to get his online certificate as an ordained minister so he could marry them. His efforts had been wasted.

Letting out a sigh that almost took tears along with it, she explained, "Uncle Don, the wedding is off, but not because of the weather. It's off because there's no groom and no maid of honor." She swallowed the growing lump in her throat. "Brandon ran off with Jessica last night."

The elderly man teetered as if knocked back by an invisible fist. His hand went to his heart. Ashley stood up and held on to him so he wouldn't fall. The last thing they needed was an elderly gentleman with a broken hip. Pulling out a chair, she helped him sit in it.

His hand shook as he reached for her hand, pulling her down into the chair beside him. "They—they ran off? Together? And left you here? Are you sure?"

Brandon's Dear-Jane note lay on the table and she pushed it toward him. Uncle Don could read the news for himself.

Standing up, she put her hands on the frosty window and leaned against it. The cold glass quickly fogged up where her hands and her breath touched it. She put her forehead against the pane. The damp cold seemed more real than what she felt inside. Her groom and her maid of honor were out there in the storm. Somewhere. Together. She hoped they were stuck in a snowbank. And she hoped they were cold. Biting cold so they'd be hurting like she was.

As her forehead numbed with the cold, she stepped back from the window. Pulling a mascara-blackened tissue out of her strapless bodice, she wiped her eyes. The action removed more of the mascara so painstakingly applied two hours earlier. She rubbed several dark splotches on the lacy bodice with manicured fingers. An hour ago, the spots would have mattered. Now, nothing mattered.

A murmur of distress mixed with sympathy signaled Uncle Don had finished reading the note. He made funny sounds while not saying anything. Ashley knew his mind was churning while looking for the right words. He often did that when he wanted to say something profound or important. He was like her wise grandfather, and she valued what he had to say. Except for now. No words could soothe her heartache.

"Ashley..." he began.

She closed her eyes and turned to face the window again, fighting to remain respectful. He was her elder and deserved to be heard even though she really wanted to run weeping to her room.

"...I'm sad for you. My heart hurts for you. But it's also happy. For you to have married that man—the one who took away your happiness on a whim—if you'd married him, your life would have been miserable. I never want that for you."

Biting her bottom lip, she struggled to hold the emotion back that was threatening to send her into an ugly crying jag. She tensed her stomach muscles. A few seconds of rigidness helped her regain her composure.

"Thanks, Uncle Don. If you don't mind, I'd like to be alone."

Old-man sounds drifted to her ears as he lifted himself from the chair. A strong hand clasped her shoulder with a tight squeeze. No words needed to be spoken. His strength and sympathy came through his touch.

He sniffed as he stood beside her, looking out the window. A moment of silence drifted between them. "I don't want to seem insensitive," he said in a higher voice than usual, "but if there's no wedding, we should pack up and get back home before we're snowed in here. Look how fast it's falling!" With one last squeeze of her shoulder, he rushed out of the room.

Ashley stared out the window again. In the whiteout conditions, nothing could be seen. Only felt. It felt cold. Empty cold. Inside her, the fire of disloyalty kindled by her two best friends was being doused by the dread and fear of facing the Colemans, Brandon's parents. Their room was down the hall from hers. She had to get home before she was stuck here with them. And Joe. Just thinking his name made her insides cringe. The thick white scene of the blizzard suddenly made her feel claustrophobic.

The scent of burning wood came from the stone fireplace in the corner of the large room, causing her to turn to look at the flames. Stockings hung from the mantle and a large wreath hung above them all. A leather sofa in front of the fireplace invited her to sit and warm herself on its cushions. Behind the sofa, white-tableclothed tables with unlit candles and fine china sat ready for the wedding party's luncheon.

She turned away from the inviting warmth in front of the fire to face the other way. The giant, ornately decorated Christmas tree stood beside an evergreen-bough arch where she and Brandon would have stood to be married. A bundle of mistletoe hung from the center of the arch. The ceremony had been so romantic last night during rehearsal. Now it taunted her, rebuking her for loving someone who didn't deserve her trust.

Reminders of her ruined wedding were everywhere. She covered her face with her hands. Her house was full of wedding presents and Brandon's furniture. She wanted away from it all but had nowhere to go that wasn't full of his memories or his stuff.

The note that broke her heart lay on a table. Brandon's best man, Joe Griffin, delivered it to her this morning. She narrowed her eyes, trying to make it burst into flames. Wishing for that superpower didn't make it come true. She didn't need x-ray vision to see the words in the note. Brandon didn't want to go through with the marriage. Their time together had been fun, but he realized he didn't love her. Not like a wife. He loved her like a sister, and it would feel funny marrying his sister. He'd found real love in the arms of Jessica.

Jessica. Her life-long friend who had always stood by her. Their long history bound them together as more than friends. It had made them sisters so naturally she'd asked her to be the maid of honor. Strange title for someone who no longer had any honor. She bit her bottom lip to steady her quivering chin.

With trembling hands, she picked up the letter. Joe's demeanor when he delivered it had made matters much worse. The unpleasant man had almost recited it, like he helped write it, and laughed after he was done reading it.

Joe was a thorn in her side. Ever since he and Brandon became friends, things had not been the same. Brandon seemed more interested in pleasing Joe than pleasing her. The two of them hung out at places that she didn't approve of and stayed out to all hours. Joe explained it away as sowing wild oats before being chained to a wife. Ashley didn't like the kind of farming he and Brandon had been doing. Brandon's sudden impulses to do things before he was married cast the first shadow. It was like he regretted his decision to propose to her. He became a little distant, but she credited it to cold feet. All grooms had cold feet, didn't they?

Her mother told her it was sacrilegious to have a wedding on Christmas Eve. They'd argued about it, but Ashley was resolute. Christmas Eve was the best time to get married. Joy was part of the season, and the holiday break made it easy for their close friends and family to come. It was the perfect time to celebrate the birth of a new family.

A gust of wind shook the building, and she turned to look at the white outside. God must have agreed with her mother. He didn't seem too pleased with her Christmas Eve wedding plans either.

Uncle Don was right. She'd better get on the road, or she'd be stuck here with the Colemans and the wedding arch. But first, one thing had to be done. Crumpling the hurtful note, she ran to the large fireplace in the corner where the flames waited to consume it. Lifting her arm to throw it in, she heard a small voice behind her.

"Are you a princess?"

Ashley spun around, searching for the source of the question. No one was in the room with her. Maybe she was imagining things. Maybe it was the voice of her childhood self. She'd wanted to be a princess all her life. She'd chosen the wedding gown because it looked like a dress she'd seen in a Disney movie. Another memory floated out from a hidden place. A cast-off dress of her mother's used to trail behind her as she pretended to be Cinderella. She'd swirl and dance around her imaginary ballroom until she was breathless and dizzy.

Her youthful memories took over her thoughts and took her away from her present self. Reaching down, she lifted the side of her full skirt and pirouetted like she had as a girl. She was a princess on the ballroom floor, dancing with her Prince Charming.

"You ARE a princess!"

The voice was closer and drew her out of her daydream. Ashley looked around and saw one blue eye peering from behind a chair near the banquet hall entrance. The voice belonged to the lodge owner's daughter, Molly. On several previous visits to the lodge, the girl would magically appear out of nowhere with a knowing look in her eyes. The little spy could be found all over the lodge, absorbing everything she could. Little seemed to get past her.

Ashley motioned for the child to come out.

The five-year-old girl edged her way around the chair. Her long blonde hair hung over her eyes as she tugged at the hem of her Christmas sweatshirt. She pointed at Ashley's head, "You have a crown!"

Reaching up, Ashley touched the tiara that held her veil. A one-sided smile moved her face. "Hi, Molly. I'm not—"

A gasp and a puzzled look came across the child's face as she tipped her head. "Why do you have black eyes?"

Ashley hurried to a table to get a napkin to wipe the mascara away. Rushing to the table where her three-tiered wedding cake sat in its sugary splendor, she grabbed a paper napkin to wipe the running mascara away. Keeping her back to the child, she murmured, "Um, my makeup got messed up." She wiped her eyes more, then turned around. "Better?"

The child nodded and skipped over to Ashley. "May I touch your crown?"

The child's pleading eyes warmed the cold emptiness inside Ashley. Taking the child's hand, they walked to the large leather sofa in front of the fireplace. "Let's sit here."

The girl bounced up and sat on the edge of the sofa. Her eyes were wide with wonder as she stared at every fold of the voluminous skirt.

Reaching behind her, Ashley pulled the long veil around her so she could sit. She pulled part of her skirt over Molly's legs when she sat beside her, lighting up the blue eyes with delight. The girl felt of the fabric between her fingers and stroked it like a treasured pet.

The girl's inquisitiveness of the fine fabric made Ashley smile. She pulled out several bobby pins before pulling the tiara off her head. Finger-combing and twisting the girl's long tresses into a knot on top of her head, Ashley applied her small pile of bobby pins to the girl's coif. Little hands were feeling around the top of her head so much, Ashley had to tell her to sit still. A squeal of dream-come-true wonder filled the banquet hall as she slid the tiara on the girl's head and spread the veil across her shoulders. The girl was transformed into a princess.

The veil drug on the floor as Molly jumped up and spun around, holding the edges of the veil out with her arms. "Look at me! I'm a princess!"

Motioning to the girl, Ashley said, "Come, let me help you so it doesn't drag on the floor so much." She wrapped the long veil around her shoulders, providing both a crown and a lacy play dress for the occasion. "There. Now you can get around better with your crown, Princess Molly."

"Am I as beautiful as you?"

Imagining how she must look with red eyes, splotchy face, and smeared makeup, the question was an easy one to answer. "You are much more beautiful than I am."

Molly ran and twirled around the floor in front of the tables. Her laughter rang through the once dreary room, filling it with the happiness of a child granted a wish.

Ashley sat back in the sofa, losing herself in the child's innocent dance. The girl knew nothing of heartbreak or betrayal. To her, the world was simple and good and all about princesses. She used to be that girl. Carefree. Joyful. Happy. That's how she expected to feel today, her wedding day. Instead, it was the day her dream died.

Her vision blurred with too many tears. She felt around on the sofa and found the napkin again. When she had her emotions under control, she found the girl standing in front of her.

"Why are you sad?" she asked softly. "You can have your crown back." Her hands went to the tiara sparkling in the firelight.

Quickly, Ashley reached out and put the girl's hands down. "The crown is yours to keep. Wear it and play with it. I hope it brings you much more happiness than it did me."

In a single moment, Ashley could see that it already had. The beaming child skipped away, the train floating out behind her like a cape.

CHAPTER 2

·▾·♥·▾·

Ashley faced the window of her room, watching the snow pile up while she tapped her toe. Her mother, Maggie, paced across the room behind her, alternating between ranting how Brandon wasn't good enough for her daughter and weeping over the loss of all the money she'd spend on the wedding. She lamented that Brandon was too arrogant, too self-centered, too...too...not good enough. And Jessica. That girl had been like one of the family, she cried out as she wailed. How could she do this to them?

Her parents had been crazy about Brandon before today. So crazy about him that they used their savings for a Mediterranean cruise to pay for the wedding. Ashley tried to talk them out of it. She had a good job and could pay for it herself, but her mother, adhering to strict customary rules, insisted that the bride's parents pay for everything. They'd saved for years for this bucket-list cruise and now it was all gone. Down the tubes on a wedding and a man who was no good.

Ashley understood her mother's rantings. She felt the same way. Inside her, confusion stirred her mix of emotions like a blender, yielding a strange concoction that was bitter to drink. Her mother's grieving for the cruise only added to Ashley's guilt. Their dream had been wasted on a flop.

Maggie's voice dragged like sandpaper over Ashley's insides. Putting her fingers in her ears and humming might drown out the sound, but it would look childish. With concentrated effort, she focused her mind on the faintly visible fir tree outside as it sparred with the pounding wind and snow. The movement of the tree was mesmerizing. Flailing against an unseen force, it almost seemed alive.

In the warm room on the other side of the window, Ashley fought her own battle. She wanted to hide, to go home to her apartment, away from everyone, but the snow was already deeper than when she was in the banquet hall. She was unable to leave. Her father wanted to stay at the lodge because of the dangerous roads. If she stayed, she'd be trapped in the lodge with people she didn't want to be around. Pushing away the twinge of panic born of claustrophobia, she turned away from looking at her icy captor howling through the tree outside.

Stuffing her hands into her jeans pockets, Ashley watched as her mother pace and complain. Looking years younger than her five-plus decades, anger lined her face as she paced murmuring to herself, pounding the air with her fists. Her dark green mother-of-the-bride dress fit her middle-aged figure well and complemented her short red hair. Ashley often wished she looked more like her mother, tall and model-like, but she took more after her father whose Asian ancestors were shorter.

Ashley wanted to say something to her mother to try to calm her down but bit her tongue. What could she say? That it was all right? It wasn't. That calling off the wedding was better than marrying and divorcing later? Not a helpful thought right now. That she'd pay back the costs of the wedding and they could go on their cruise? That was a good place to start.

Before she could utter the words, a loving arm went around her shoulders, pulling her close. Her father, Randy, with his quiet strength and cool head, blocked out her mother's misery and brought comfort to her. She leaned against his soft sweatshirt, allowing his strength to soothe her heartache.

"It's okay, baby," he whispered in her ear. "Let her vent. She doesn't mean a word of it." He gave her a peck on the cheek, like he'd done for all her twenty-six years. That peck meant he loved her and would take care of things. "Don't worry. Everything will work out. It just seems bad now."

A loud knock at the door interrupted Maggie's ranting. She opened the door a little and Joe stuck his head in. "Hi, folks! How's it going in here?"

With a roll of her eyes, Maggie admitted the man whose company was desired by no one. He pushed the door shut and faced his unwilling audience.

Ashley rubbed her temples. "What do you want, Joe?" she said in a tone of voice that might give him the hint to leave.

He lifted his chin and narrowed his eyes. "Not in a good mood. That's understandable." He nodded as if he understood. "I have just the cure for you. You know all that champagne and wine. Let's break it out and have a big party. We can christen this dumpy lodge the Heartbreak Hotel. Who's with me?" He held his arms and grin wide.

In the blink of an eye, Maggie put her tear-stained face into his. "Your cure is to party and get drunk?" She waited a split second, giving him a slit to provide an answer, but from the look on the stunned man's face, his brain didn't work that fast. "This wedding is a dry one. Some of the guests have had problems with alcohol in the past. To prevent temptation and falling off the wagon, it was banned."

"Banned? Does that mean there's no wine or champagne?" His eyes glazed over. "I've never heard of a wedding without wine."

"Now you have." Maggie reached around him and opened the door. "Take your alcoholism and get out of here!"

Joe's mouth opened and closed a time or two as his face reddened. "I'm not an alcoholic! I'm trying to put a happy end to this fiasco."

With a growl befitting a bear about to attack, Maggie replied, "You can either leave, or you can get thrown out. Which do you prefer?"

He looked at Ashley with raised eyebrows and an are-you-going-to-let-her-do-this-to-me look.

She stared back at him through narrowed eyes without moving a muscle.

Shaking his head and muttering something about how dull the lodge was, he moved toward the door, but stopped. "Oh yeah, I'm supposed to tell you the owner of this dump wants to talk to you."

Ashley pushed her father's arm away. "This is not a dump! Don't you dare talk like that."

Emoting a look of innocence, he shrugged and said, "Sorry," before he left.

Maggie put an exclamation mark on the issue with a slam of the door. "There's the reason why there's no wedding. That guy is poison. To him, everything must be entertaining. If it's not, he wants out. He corrupted Brandon against you."

Finding no reason to disagree, Ashley nodded her head as she sat on the edge of the bed. "You're right, Mom. Since Brandon met him, everything has seemed out of sorts. He's a bad influence."

The door of the room burst open, causing Ashley to jump. Her teenage brother Mason came running in, waving her veil in the air. "Guess what I found some girl playing with." He threw out his chest as he shook the veil at Ashley. "I got it back for you."

Maggie grabbed the veil from him. "A girl was playing with it? I bet she stole the key from the desk and got in your room. You should see if anything else was taken, Ashley. Imagine that. A hoodlum running around here." She took it to the bed and smoothed it out. "I KNEW we should have had a church wedding instead of one in this broken-down lodge."

"Everybody, stop!" Ashley screamed out. She pinched her lips together to keep harsher words from escaping. "This is not a broken-down lodge! This is a really nice place! I'm tired of everyone insulting my favorite place to be when I need time away from the noise and rush of Denver."

A smug look shaped Maggie's face. "Oh Ashley, quit being such a drama queen. It's nice enough, but it's no Four Seasons Hotel. If you'd been married in our church, we wouldn't be stuck here on the side of a mountain in a snowstorm."

Randy pulled his wife into his arms. "Maggie, settle down! You're close to saying hurtful things that you'll regret later."

Wiping away as much stress as she could, Ashley tried to calm her wildly beating heart. Her mind wobbled on the edge of a screaming fit, and there was a strong wind at her back. It was a place she'd rarely been before. Only fear of damaging valuable relationships kept her struggling to keep her balance. She took a deep breath and took a step back from the edge. "Look, I gave my veil to Molly because it made her happy. She's a sweet little girl, and she wanted to be a princess. I let her try it on and she had such a good time with it, I let her keep it. You shouldn't have taken it away from her, Mason."

Pushing Randy away, Maggie cried out, "I can't believe you'd give your veil away. You know how much this cost? We might could return it for a refund." She turned away. "It's just like you to not care about how much things cost. Never mind it would pay for several days in a hotel in Greece." She picked up the veil and held it next to her.

With a heavy sigh, Randy shook his head. "Maggie, could we forget about that for now? This is about Ashley, not our trip. Think of how this makes her feel. Like she's less important than a cruise."

"A bucket-list cruise!" Maggie crossed her arms and looked away, blinking rapidly.

Ashley gritted her teeth. The money for that stupid cruise was the beached whale in the room. A formal wedding at her favorite getaway seemed like a good idea at one time. Standing on its shattered ruins, she wished she'd acquiesced to her mother's wishes and gotten married in a church. Or better yet, she should have eloped and avoided all this mess.

The regrets would have to wait until later. All that mattered now was the money. "Mom, I promise I will pay you back. All of it. As soon as I get home and transfer the money. You don't need to worry about it anymore. Book your cruise and make your plans."

One issue down, one to go. Ashley took the veil from her mother's reluctant hands. "Mason, the veil belongs to Molly. You shouldn't have taken it away from her. I'd appreciate it if you'd take it back. Apologize and tell her you didn't know."

Mason struck the pose of an oppressed teen, doing a dance of guilt. "Oh...yeah...put all the blame on me. Well, you should have told me you gave it to her. How was I to know? Never mind that I was saving your stuff for you. I thought she stole it. No. Make me the bad guy. Again." He threw himself, pouty face and all, into a slump in the one chair in the room. "I never do anything right."

Rubbing her fingers over the rhinestones on the tiara, Ashley asked, "Did she cry?"

Nodding his head while rolling his eyes, Mason deflected the question. "Not my fault. You didn't tell me you gave it to her." He inserted his earbuds and tuned out.

Putting her free hand over her face, she rubbed at the tension building in her temples. Poor Molly. Having the veil and her new identity ripped away must have been hurtful. She held on to her chin to keep it from quivering too much. Tears for a sad little girl would open the floodgates on the overfilled reservoir. The flood would be uncontrollable.

Rather than argue with her sulking brother, she said, "Never mind. I'll take it to her." She ran her hand through her hair. "Dad, I think we should go see David. He probably wants to talk about—" She had no idea.

Throwing her red hair back away from her face, Maggie replied, "The cheapskate that owns this place should give us a full refund. Even if the wedding weren't off, no one can get here because of the weather. Why should we pay for renting the lodge when no one is here?"

The fire in Ashley took over as the volcano of her rage blew its top. "He's not a cheapskate! He's a very nice man!" she yelled at the top of her voice. "Brandon is the one who's not nice. You want your money back? Sue the bum for breach of promise! Sue him for all he's worth! Then you can cruise around the world two or three times. Would you be happy then?"

Randy hustled to stand between the two women who were squared off like bull elk. He held his arms wide to keep them apart as he said, "Now, now, Maggie. We can't expect to get a refund. The weather. Brandon. All of it was beyond the lodge owner's control. He's already bought the food, and he turned away other reservations. We can't expect him to eat those costs."

Maggie let out a disgusted sound. "Yes, we can. It's part of doing business."

Ashley jumped at her mother, but she was held back by Randy's arm. "That's crazy! You know nothing about running a business. All you care about is the money and taking a vacation! I wish I'd never let you talk me into letting you pay for this stupid wedding. I can't let an innocent bystander get hurt by my stupid decision to marry—" The words stuck in her throat, strangling her from going on.

"You're right! Then that worthless Brandon owes me the money! I'll sue him! And I'll sue Jessica too! How could she do such a thing? She was like one of the family!"

The tears welled up in Maggie's eyes and her face scrunched up right before her wailing started. Randy quickly grabbed her and pulled her into his arms. "This has gone on long enough. Let's go to our room, Maggie, so you can have a good cry. Ashley, I'll talk to you in a little while."

The tension hung in the air like stinking cigar smoke. Ashley looked at the veil and crown in her hand, the catalyst of the argument. She looked at her brother who started it all by taking it away from Molly. Mason sat in the chair, one ear bud out and one eye on the action. The side of his mouth was up, and his eyes had a look like he was making bets with himself over who the winner of the fight would be.

"Come on, Mason," Randy said when he reached the door.

Mason grumbled something about the fight was just getting good. He put the earbud back in and drug his feet on the way out.

Flinging the veil on the bed, Ashley released the pent-up tears in private. Her dreams had caused this fiasco. Her dreams of an intimate Christmas Eve wedding had blown up in her face. She should have settled for a low-expense, low-hubbub, face-saving elopement. But her man didn't love her. No matter. What was done was done. It wouldn't happen again because she wouldn't let herself be so dumb as to fall in love again.

She'd learned her lesson. Maybe a single life was the best way to live. A master's degree in marketing and a great job made her self-sufficient. From now on, her career would be her priority. Christmas would be for religious purposes only. Her family could provide moral support if she ever needed it. No one else was necessary. Freedom was hers. If loneliness hit, a dog would suffice. Dogs were loyal and faithful. No dog would run off on a night like last night.

She felt better. Her future was planned. All that was left was deciding whether to give in to the grief and cry a river of tears over the humiliation of being left at the altar or to let her anger out and destroy something. Crying would be easy, but she didn't want to surrender the emotional control. She touched the fabric of her gown and wondered how easy it would be to tear it to pieces.

CHAPTER 3

⸱▾⸱▾⸱

The flames in the large stone fireplace roared back to life when David Larson stoked the ashes and added more firewood. In the nearby chair, Molly still sniffled over the loss of her status symbol as a princess. She rubbed an eye with her fist and curled into a ball. She'd come in screaming to him about someone stealing her crown. She claimed the princess gave it to her. He didn't know what that meant. All he knew was she didn't own a crown.

David swept up the bits of bark on the floor and threw them into the fire. The longing for his wife Monica to take care of their pouting daughter was almost overwhelming, but the responsibility fell on him. Everything fell on him four years ago when a tragic car accident took his wife away.

Christmas had been Monica's favorite holiday. She had always decorated their inn with greens, lights, joy, and laughter. He still had the decorations and lights, but nothing could replace her childlike happiness and delight in the holiday season. Since her passing, Christmas was a time of mourning. Everything reminded him of what he'd lost. But for Molly's sake, he had to keep up a happy charade. Monica would be furious at him if he ruined the season for her.

He surveyed the banquet hall of his inn. His small staff had worked for hours to set up the tables, the china, the arch, and all the other trimmings for the wedding. He hadn't wanted to host the event in the first place. Getting married on Christmas Eve was a bad idea.

When his regular customer Ashley Chen begged to rent the inn for her wedding, he told her no at first. Her pleading got so intense that he found it hard to turn her away. Instead, he quoted a price so high he was sure she'd turn it down. She didn't blink an eye, but immediately accepted. He immediately regretted it. Not because he'd have to take away his staff's holidays and promise them extra money. Not because he minded the business. He regretted it because he didn't want to lose a good customer. Her visits might end if she married. But it was more than that. He didn't want to admit it to anyone, but he always looked forward to her visits. Something about her lightened his heart and made him smile more.

Brett Schultz brought in another armload of firewood and placed it in the wood bin next to the fireplace. As he brushed the snow off his coat, he remarked to David, "Glad you sent everyone home early. It's coming down fast and hard out there." The snow sticking to his wool stocking hat began to disappear.

"Better bring in more wood." David picked up the poker and stirred the logs around. "If the electricity goes off, we'll need lots of it. Our underground utilities may save us for a while, but no telling what the lines are like beyond that."

"We got lanterns in the shed, plus a few cots. If we lose power, sleeping in front of the fireplace will be warmer than in the rooms."

David ran his fingers through his hair. "I should have never agreed to having this crazy wedding. We both knew that guy was playing her for a fool."

Taking off his gloves and putting them under his arm, Brett warmed his hands in front of the fire. "You should have told her about it when I caught him in bed with that other woman a few months ago."

"It isn't my place to tell her her fiancée is a two-timing scumbag. I'm just the lodge owner."

"But it's a little more, ain't it," Brett said as he gave his boss a wink. "I see how you look at her."

David felt his face grow hot and it wasn't from the fire. "You're seeing things," he mumbled as he turned away to get another log.

Brett chuckled as he put his gloves back on and pulled his hat farther down over his ears "With the way the snow is piling up, the power'll go off anytime now. I'll keep hauling wood. Tell Linda I'll help her clean up this room when I get done." Wet footprints stayed behind when he left for more wood.

"Daddy," Molly whined from the chair. "What did Brett mean when he said he saw how you look at her? Who was he talking about?"

David grumbled under his breath. One of these days he'd learn not to say anything within her keen hearing range. Nothing got past her and with her five-year-old imagination, no telling what or who would hear about it. "Brett was being silly. It was nothing. Why don't you go play in your room?"

The lights blinked, and he was glad for the distraction. It also signaled trouble. No power meant planning contingencies. This blasted wedding. If it were any other Christmas Eve, he and Molly would camp out in front of the fireplace, roast hot dogs, and smores. Easy. But with eight guests checked in, he'd have to think of something else. The restaurant kitchen and freezer were filled with wedding food, but little of it could be stuck on the end of a stick and heated up. If all else failed, they could pig out on the elaborate wedding cake delivered right before the storm hit.

With more force than he intended, he threw another log on the fire. Sparks flew outward, causing him to jump back and brush the embers back into the fireplace.

He had to talk to Ashley and her father about the cancellation of the wedding. The bills for food, personnel, and decorations had already been accrued and had to be covered. No refunds were possible He was firm on that. He used his hand to iron out the worry furrows on his brow. He would never book anything over Christmas again, no matter how good the money.

The clinking of silverware and the stacking of china beat in time with the crackling fire. Linda Schultz was taking up the china, silverware, and decorations they'd placed so carefully the day before. She wiped each plate and carefully packed them away in the wooden boxes on her trolley cart.

Brett and Linda were more than part of his staff. They were his best friends and confidantes. Living contentedly in a little log cabin behind the lodge, they all formed the family who ran the Spruce Canyon Lodge.

David went to the windows and watched the raging storm as his own internal storm raged. Why had he let her sensitive dark eyes coerce him into a Christmas wedding? Why did a tilt of her beautiful head make him agree to host the event? He was a fool. Keeping the lodge going in memory of his wife's love for the place wasn't enough to make it a success. His father-in-law was right. He had no head for business. He should sell the place and find a real job. For Molly's sake.

The lights blinked again, bringing his self-flagellation to an end. With strong swipes of his arms, he pulled heavy drapes across the windows that ran the length of the room. The room became darker and warmer with the frosty window panes blocked. He checked the water in the large Christmas tree before moving to help clear the tables. He took a corner of a white tablecloth and folded it. At least there'd be no extra laundry duties tomorrow. Or should he wash them anyway? He'd let Linda decide.

"No surprise the wedding is off."

David looked up at Linda who gave him a knowing look. "The only ones surprised are the wedding party. Other than the one guy."

"It's a shame it got this far. A waste of time and money."

Linda clicked her tongue. "If the bride had asked us, we could have told her he was a philanderer. And a shameless one to boot."

Stacking plates in the storage box, David sighed. "Love is blind."

"Or in this case, blind and stupid."

"Now, Linda, we've all been that at one time or another. Ashley's no—" Reaching for another tablecloth, a movement caught David's eye. Ashley and Randy stood timidly at the entrance of the banquet hall. Heat rushed up his neck into his face. From the looks of his uncomfortable guests they may have overheard the short conversation.

Ashley had jeans and a sweatshirt on, but her father was dressed in his good suit. Draped over Ashley's arm was a white veil and tiara. They both looked at the floor and shifted from foot to foot like they'd rather be anywhere in the world but here.

David felt the same.

Motioning for them to go sit on the sofa in front of the fireplace, he handed the tablecloth to Linda. "Wish me luck." A whispered wish followed him as he made his way to the fireplace. He desperately missed his wife in moments like these. She'd had the business savvy that made her efficient in dealing with their customers. Firm, but courteous. A negotiator like none other. All the skills he was working to develop but he had a long way to go.

Firm. Be firm, he urged his inner self.

Molly sat up in the chair when she saw Ashley come around the corner to the sofa. Her eyes widened with the unmistakable look of longing as she stared at the veil. Her heart's desire was plainly evident.

Ashley bent down and put the tiara on Molly's head. "Guess what I found? Your crown! Here you go, Princess Molly." She adjusted the tiara and tulle, then pulled the short veil down over the blissful face.

As with any good dad, David's heart lightened at the sight of his daughter's overjoyed face. One issue was cleared up. His daughter was a princess again. "Thank Miss Chen for the generous gift, Princess Molly."

With a voice that conveyed her inner joy, Molly replied, "Thank you for the crown, Princess Miss Chen! Will you tell my daddy that I can keep it?"

Ashley laughed as she said, "I'll tell him if he or anyone else takes it away from you, they'll be banished to the kingdom of the trolls."

Molly glared at her father and shook a finger at him. "Did you hear that, Daddy?"

A memory of her mother on their wedding day flashed through David's mind. His beautiful bride had passed her looks on to her daughter. Always happy to play along, David took a step back and put a fist to his chest. "The kingdom of the trolls? Oh, please, not there, Your Highness! You can keep the crown, Princess, just don't send me to the trolls!" He gave her a quick hug and told her to go play in her room while he tended to business.

Molly jumped off the chair and embraced Ashley's legs. Looking straight up, she said, "I wanted to be a princess all my life and now I am." With a little pirouette, she held out the veil and ran to one end of the sofa before turning and running between David and Ashley and out the door. Her laughter bounced back at them as she went.

The theatrics having ended, David invited Ashley and Randy to sit. He sat in Molly's chair. Not knowing how to exactly start this conversation, he cleared his throat while his mind churned. All he heard was "be firm" echoing over other more logical thoughts.

Randy saved David from the first move. "I know your cancellation policy at this late date doesn't allow for a refund. However, if there's anything you could do for us, we'd be grateful."

Ashley put her arm on her father's arm. "No, Dad, that's not fair." She moved to the edge of the sofa so she could look at David straight on. "We paid to rent the inn for my wedding and Christmas Day. We'll stay the night, then leave tomorrow morning. Your staff can go home to spend Christmas Day with their families." She hung her head. Her voice broke as she said, "Mom was right. I was crazy to think a Christmas Eve wedding was a good idea."

Rubbing his palms along his thighs, David wished he could rub away her hurt. She was a nice lady and very attractive. Her dark eyes and flawless skin made her look sophisticated and beautiful. For a split second, he felt a tug on his heartstrings, but quickly dismissed it. Her job as a marketing director for a Fortune 500 company meant she met lots of people. She'd have no trouble finding someone else to love her after the hurt eased. He was nothing but a small lodge owner. No big deal.

He almost envied her. His was a solitary life, watching others in love while he and his staff made them comfortable. The loss of Monica had left a big hole in his heart, filled only by watching Molly grow into a woman like her mother. His employees had been with him through thick and thin. They were his closest family other than Molly.

A light cough from Randy brought him out of his daydream. Heat rose from his chest into his neck and face. He ran his hand through his hair. "Um, no, I can't refund any money. We're past the cancellation date. I'm sorry."

Randy leaned forward. "How about a refund for Christmas night? We're giving you 24 hours' notice of that cancellation."

"Dad!" Ashley said out of the side of her mouth. "Stop it! I told you I'd pay you back so don't make a big deal out of this. Business is business." She turned toward David and smiled as if nothing were wrong. "Don't mind him. I know you can't refund anything, and I understand completely. We also wanted you to know that we'll be leaving this afternoon. My mother and I insist..." she held up her hand to stop her father from speaking, "...that we get home before the storm gets any worse."

David tapped his fingertips together. "That might be a problem," he said slowly. "The State Patrol called a little bit ago. Unless this storm lets up soon, the interstate is likely to be closed due to avalanches and ice. I wouldn't be surprised if it was closed already. You may have to stay here until the storm passes and the highways cleared." David looked at the two whose eyes were as wide as their mouths. To deliver the last blow, he added, "You may be stuck here until the day after Christmas."

Randy stood quickly. "We should leave now. Ashley, go get your mother and brother. Tell them we're headed back before it gets any worse."

As bad as he wanted a private Christmas with Molly, he knew it shouldn't happen. The safety of his guests was the top priority. Blocking their way, David held out his hand. "Not a good idea. It's very hazardous out there. Look, you've paid for your rooms and the meals. Everything is set for you to enjoy the holiday here. There's no sense in driving in a blizzard when you've got a place that's warm and comfortable. Stay safe by staying here."

Ashley looked like a woman walking the plank. "But the Colemans are here," she whispered through her clenched teeth. "It's very uncomfortable for all of us to be together in one place. We were hoping to avoid them by leaving now."

David hadn't thought about that. The bride's family eating with the missing groom's family. Conflicts had started over lesser things. He didn't want to spend Christmas mediating peace between warring factions. Maybe between he and Brett and Linda, they could come up with a plan to put plenty of space between them.

The phone buzzed in his pocket, a timely interruption. He excused himself as he went into the hallway. The State Patrol was calling again to provide an update. After he hung up, he tapped his fingertips on the back of the phone. While he might not avoid a family feud, he might be able to wrestle a small peace offering in this mess.

David walked back to the pair on the couch and sat in his formerly warm chair. "That was the State Patrol saying the roads are closed and asking if we had room to house stranded travelers they find on the interstate. I'll tell you what I'll do for you. If you'll let me rent the rooms you have reserved for your guests, I'll refund that part of your money. The menu we planned for you, we'll share with any travelers they bring. After the storm and I get everything settled, I might be able to refund a little of that, but not all. And I won't guarantee it, but I'll do my best to work something reasonable out for both of us."

Ashley nodded. "That sounds more than fair. Right, Dad?"

David held up his hand to prevent the deal ending prematurely. "One more thing. My housecleaning staff and waitresses can't make it through the snow. Since we're shorthanded, you may have to make your own beds, and your rooms won't be cleaned every day. I'm sorry."

Ashley smiled. "That's no problem, If that's all that we need to do to help, we're good."

Randy held his hand out. "Agreed."

They all stood up, and the men shook hands. As David took Ashley's offered hand, he felt a sparkle run up his arm. He quickly looked down, hoping she hadn't seen a change in his face. Pulling his hand away, he offered an additional olive branch. "Maybe with other people here, it will be less awkward between you and the Colemans."

Ashley held up both hands with crossed fingers.

Out of the corner of his eye, David saw Linda motioning from the dining room. "Oh by the way," he told them. "Lunch is ready. We'll be serving the pork marsala as planned. Would you mind inviting your family down to eat? I'll ask the Colemans to come down after you're done."

For the first time that day, David watched Ashley's eyes light up. She looked pretty despite her slightly puffy eyes and mussed hair. His heart beat a little faster as he watched her and her father go down the hallway.

CHAPTER 4

✦·❦·✦·❦·✦

B y mid-afternoon, Ashley had cried her grief out, dried her tears, and stayed in her room long enough to let her eyes unswell and unredden. The world kept turning although from the looks outside, time had gone back to the Ice Age. She'd apologized to her mother who apologized back. All was well again between them. Only one distasteful wedding item remained.

Before she confronted the Colemans, she needed some time with her Uncle Don. His words of wisdom and strength got her through the rough spots during high school and college. His nonjudgmental guidance helped her find the right answers when they were unclear to her.

He answered the door looking bleary-eyed.

"I woke you from a nap," she said.

Clearing his throat, he smiled and pulled her inside. "No matter. Just catching a nap before supper." He laughed. "Without TV to watch, not much to do other than sleep."

"They have a small library by the reception desk. I'll show it to you."

He nodded as he sat in the one chair and invited her to sit on the bed. "What's on your mind?"

Finding a loose thread on the comforter, she played with it while she tried to think of how to say what she was thinking. "Seen the Colemans this morning?"

"No. Have you?"

She shook her head.

"And you're afraid to?"

She wiggled back and forth. "Not really afraid. Just dreading that initial contact."

"Being uncomfortable is natural. Just do it and get it over with. They're probably as nervous as you. Make the first move." He leaned forward, looking at her intently. "Gives you the advantage to pick your battlefield. Or your place for peace talks. Taking the initiative gives you lead."

Her uncle's twinkling eyes and wink brought a smile to her face.

"Go get 'em, girl. You can do it."

Rising, she gave his bald head a quick kiss. "Thanks, Uncle Don. I needed the pep talk." She took a deep breath of courage and marched out the door.

A few minutes later, Ashley's mouth went dry as she stood in front of the room of her not-to-be in-laws. Her heart pounded so hard it made her locket bounce faintly against her shirt. It had to be done. An appropriate time would never come for this unpleasant chore. Waiting would make it worse. Better to face it here out of view of other people than bumping into them when others were around.

A deep cleansing breath helped her shaking hands. She knocked at the door and waited for the unknown. Would they invite her in or slam the door in her face? Would they blame her for running Brandon off? If they wanted to make a scene, they'd have to do it here out of sight of her parents. Her mother's mindset would only add gas to the flames, and the explosion would be felt by everyone. Being trapped in the lodge didn't allow room for a Hatfield-and-McCoy feud between families. The demilitarized zone was only the width of the hallway.

The Colemans' door remained closed. Her roiling thoughts made her lose track of time. Should she knock again, or was it too soon? She didn't want to seem eager, but she wanted this over with as soon as possible. Her feet danced with impatience until she lifted her fist to knock again. The sound of a lock being undone made her pause.

Opening the door only a crack, Bob Coleman peeked out. "Oh!" He shut the door slightly, said something Ashley couldn't make out, then opened the door only enough to slip out. "I didn't expect to see you."

Ashley had always admired this man who would have been her father-in-law. He was a lot like her dad. Tall and distinguished looking, he was as kind and down-to-earth as any wanna-be saint. She'd hoped Brandon would age and mature like his dad. She wanted to watch the transformation up close over the years. Instead he'd transformed into a traitor.

With a soft nudge, Bob directed her down the hallway a little. "Rhonda has cried all morning. I can't figure out what was in Brandon's mind to do what he's done. Do you think Jessica seduced him? They didn't seem overly attentive to each other last night. Maybe something happened after we went to bed."

Words of anger shot up from her stomach, ready to cover this man with verbal acid. Ashley caught the auditory flood at the last millisecond or the man would have been thoroughly burned. Putting the blame on her best friend instead of on his son seemed like a cheap shot. How dare he imply her best friend would do such a thing! But Jessica wasn't her best friend any more. She was last night, but not today. Maybe it was her fault. Maybe it wasn't. It really didn't matter. Nothing Bob said would justify why his lousy son deserted his bride on their wedding day.

Somehow the voice of reason pushed back Ashley's need to wreak vengeance on the gentle man. The sad look in his eyes revealed the internal struggle he was wrestling with, looking for logic in his son's actions. He didn't understand it any more than she did. It wasn't the time to point fingers or place blame. Some sort of truce needed to be reached to retain peace until they left this rustic prison. Otherwise, lines would be drawn, war would break out, and it would be ugly.

Keeping her eyes focused on something other than Bob lest she lose control of her tongue, Ashley asked quickly, "You know we're stuck here?"

Bob nodded. "David came by a little bit ago."

"Since we're stuck in close quarters because of the storm, I think we should set our feelings aside. Talking about who's to blame or who did what to whom is off limits. There'll be time to toss grenades and hate each other after we get home."

Crossing his arms, Bob nodded. "Agreed."

"I've made the rules clear to my parents, and I hope you and Rhonda will abide by them too for the sake of the Christmas season. David says the State Patrol will be bringing stranded travelers here, and he may need our help in taking care of things like serving food, making our own beds, and stuff like that. Most of his workers can't make it in so he's shorthanded."

Bob rubbed the back of his neck. "Look, I'd be happy to do what I can, but Rhonda is in no shape to do anything. She's so upset with Brandon. When she heard the roads were closed, she went into hysterics wondering where he is. He may be stuck in a snowbank somewhere, freezing to death. She keeps insisting someone go look for him. It's all I can do to keep her calmed down. I don't think I can help with anyone else. I have my hands full. I hope you will understand if we stay in our room."

Oh sure, she thought. She was the one left at the altar by Brandon. The one footing the bill for this fiasco. The one whose world was upside down. But she had to be the one who understood everyone else's needs. The one volunteering to help stranded travelers. The one keeping people calm so combat didn't break out. Pile it on. She'd ask Uncle Don how stepping up gave her control. As far as she could tell, it meant she did all the work.

"Do what you think best, Bob."

She looked down at her engagement ring. The two-carat diamond was circled by other smaller diamonds. She loved the ring. The hallway lights made it sparkle. Like a magpie, she'd always been drawn to sparkly things. The symbol of Brandon's love was supposed to stay on her finger until she was old and gray. Her heart had been set on it. But his love was gone. The ring had no symbolism attached to it anymore. Other than she really loved it.

Closing her eyes, she slipped the ring off and held it out. "Here. Give this to Brandon when you see him." The seconds passed as she held it there. She opened her eyes to see him staring at the ring between them.

Taking a deep breath, he said quietly, "Why be hasty? Brandon will come around and you'll work things out and—"

"No! He lied to me. There's no going back." She grabbed his hand and stuffed the ring into it.

"When we find him, we'll talk some sense into him. It's that crazy Joe that's messed him up so bad."

She shook her head. "Joe started him down this path, but he's the one who decided to keep walking. No, it's over. I'm sorry." Turning, she ran down the hallway away from her dream of being Mrs. Coleman. Away from all she loved and wanted to be. Misery overwhelmed her and forced her eyes to blur with tears. Reaching her room, she fumbled with the key. Unable to see, she couldn't get the key in to unlock the door. More distress caused more tears.

"Here, let me help," came the gentle voice of David. He took the key from her hand and opened the door.

A whispered thanks was all she could manage before wiping her eyes and clearing the lump in her throat. "Did you need something?"

'I came to help you move into the—" he ran his hand through his hair and bit his bottom lip—"move you into the best room we have."

The Honeymoon Suite. That's what he was trying not to say. Only with her in it, it wouldn't be the Honeymoon Suite. It would be the Suite for the Brokenhearted.

He moved slightly and cleared his throat. "I thought you might enjoy relaxing in the hot tub while we still have electricity. Nothing much is visible out the windows, but the fireplace is gas and will add some comforting ambience, I think." He paused, staring at her for something.

An answer. He wanted an answer. "That would be nice. Thank you."

He pulled a key out of his pocket and gave it to her. "You go now. I'll move your things."

She shook her head as she began to get her coat off the hanger. Most of her stuff was already packed in anticipation of going home, but her wedding dress and undergarments were heaped on the bed. Her makeup and toiletries lay strewn across the bathroom counter where they'd been left when the note was delivered. Soiled tissues were scattered across the floor where she'd thoughtlessly tossed them.

"Sorry for the mess," she murmured as she bent to pick up the discarded tissues. Spotting her lacy bodysuit draped over the edge of the bed, she quickly hid it under the shirt of her wedding dress. "I wasn't expecting company."

"I don't mean to intrude." He moved the one packed suitcase near the door. "I realize you must be in a fragile state. I thought you might need some help." He shoved his hands into his pockets and looked at the floor.

His thoughtfulness spread a small smile on Ashley's face. He was the only one thinking of how she felt. For a tall woodsy man, he had a gentle heart. She liked that. And she liked him.

"Sounds wonderful," she said as she got the garment bag for her wedding dress. The bag looked tiny next to the mountain of organza that covered the top of the bed. Starting with the easy part, she got the bodice on the hanger and inside the bag.

David cleared his throat. "Did I tell you thanks for giving Molly your veil? I've never seen her so happy over anything. I'm sure it was expensive. Won't you let me pay you for it?"

Shaking her head while concentrating on pushing the skirt of the gown into the bag, she replied, "No. It's my gift to her." With each push to get her gown back into the garment bag that once held it, the volume seemed to grow. The more she pushed and tucked the full skirt into the bag, the more was outside the bag.

With a smile in his voice, he asked, "Need help?"

"No, but thanks." She repositioned her self beside the gown and the partially packed bag. Gathering up a handful of organza, she pushed it into the bag, but it seemed to spring back out. "I changed my mind. I need a hand."

With David holding the bag in place, she could gather the fabric and fold it into the bag. Slowly the volume outside the bag grew less and with one final tuck-and-shove, it all went in there. David lay on the bag while she zipped it up.

Standing up, both were out of breath from the struggle. He gave her sideways glance. "You know when you unzip that bag, you better stand back. That dress is going to explode out of there."

The mental image of the dress erupting out of the bag like pyroclastic blast from a volcano made her laugh. "Maybe I should write a warning on the bag. Caution, open with care."

A silent laugh shook David's shoulders until it couldn't be contained anymore. His laughter echoed through the room. The sound made Ashley join him in the jollity, and it felt good.

Settling down, he picked up an empty luggage bag. "What goes in this one?"

"I'll take care of it," she said as she took it from him and went into the bathroom. Makeup, nail polish, hair styling gels, and other beauty accoutrements covered the countertop. Opening the bag, she used her arm to sweep everything off the countertop into it. Organization was the least of her priorities right now. She'd deal with it later. Taking a quick glance around to make sure she had it all, she carried the bag to the bed.

David had the large garment bag over one shoulder and her suitcase in his hand. "Ready?"

As they walked to the other end of the hallway, she tried to clear her mind. Her bones ached with stress, her muscles felt weak, and her mind was dull. Time in a hot tub sounded luxurious.

David's phone sounded out as Ashley unlocked the door to the Brokenhearted Suite. She didn't wait for him but went in and went to the window. Whiteout. Nothing but white emptiness. An occasional lull in the wind gave a glimpse of the pine trees close by. The world was still out there, just obscured by the thick snowfall.

David sat her luggage on the bed and hung the garment bag in the closet. When he started the fireplace, the flames reflected in the window glass, giving the room a soft orange glow. Giving her a soft smile, he said, "That should warm it up in here."

Excusing himself, he checked his phone and listened to a voice mail as he walked toward the door. Hanging up, he let out a groan. "The State Patrol is on their way with several cars of stranded people. I need to tell Linda to prepare for more guests. I need to get that room cleaned and ready. Brett should make sure the parking lot is cleared enough for the extra cars. And to bring in more wood. I need to check the generator to make sure it has plenty of fuel."

As if suddenly remembering she was there, he looked at her. "I'm sorry. Those are not your problems. Here let me start the hot tub for you." He turned, went to the tub that sat on a raised area, and punched a button. The clean, clear water stirred and hummed. "Give it a few minutes to warm up a little more. The buttons are self-explanatory, so you can turn the jets on however you like."

Ashley stared at him. He seemed cloaked in kindness and caring for his guests, yet his stooped shoulders suggested burdens unseen. Their few moments of merriment were past, pulled away by the duties at hand. Few things tugged at her heart as much as people in need. "You want some help?"

A blank look crossed his face. "Help?" Then his brown eyes widened. "No, I couldn't impose on a guest. You've been through enough. Relax. Have a good soak. You'll feel better afterwards. I'll take care—"

A loud knock on the door frame made them both turn around. Joe stood in the doorway, looking like the cat who ate the canary. "Hey, glad I found you together. Could we get some beer or something to help pass the time? Come on, Ashley, you can't expect us to sit around all day. It's pretty boring here with no TV or music or movies."

"Who is 'we'?" Ashley asked, suspecting he referred only to himself.

Joe waved his hands in the air. "Everybody!"

She turned her head as her eyes rolled. "Once you get started on the beer, there'll be no stopping you, and I don't want to be stuck here with a drunk." She walked over to him to stare him square in the face. "If you need something to do, I'm sure David can provide you with a snow shovel. Additional guests are coming, and someone should shovel off the steps out front."

Joe's face reddened. "Now, wait a minute! I'm a paying guest here. It's not my job to do it!"

Walking closer to him, she lowered her voice. "I'm the one footing the bill. I'm the one who says what you can and cannot do. I told David we'd all pitch in and help out. Here's you chance to get a good workout. Strengthen those arm muscles. It'll keep you from being bored. What do you say? Up to the task, Mr. He Man?"

Joe stepped back and shook his finger at her. "You're a slave driver!" He rushed back down the hallway, giving one quick look behind to see if she was following.

A laugh busted out of her gut when she shut the door. "That should keep him out of your hair for a little while."

Joining in her laughter, David nodded. "Thanks. I'm getting tired of listening to him wanting me to sneak him a bottle or two. I told him it was in our contract, no alcohol. Said he wanted the free stuff meant for weddings. He's cheap and obnoxious, but you told him off good." He looked at the floor. "But seriously, if I can help you with anything, please ask."

Her heart felt a prick of warmth. The only person who seemed concerned about her feelings was David, and he hardly knew her. The ones who knew her best were more concerned about money and Brandon than her. And Brandon, who by rights should care the most, didn't care at all. Knowing that someone...anyone...cared about her made her eyes blur again. She blinked hard to keep them from running away.

Sticking her hands in her jeans, she looked at her feet. "I meant what I said. I'd like to help you. It would give me something to focus on other than myself."

She looked up at him. His light brown eyes stared at her longer than she expected. He seemed to want to see in to her soul, but she wasn't ready to expose it to him. She looked away.

"Come find me when you're ready," he said tenderly. "But first, take your time here."

He turned to go, then stopped in his tracks. "Molly! How long have you been spying?"

A blonde head popped around the door. The girl turned suddenly shy at being caught where she shouldn't have been. Twisting her foot, her arms, and her shirt into a knot, she gave him a reason for her presence. "I was looking for you. Aunt Linda wants to know how many people will be eating here tonight." She sidled over to her dad and looked up at with big blue eyes and whispered, "She says you're sweet on Ashley."

Ashley felt her mouth drop open as Molly gave her a smile.

With a face turning every shade of red, David took his daughter by the upper arm, then turned to Ashley but didn't make eye contact. "My apologies for the intrusion." They left quickly.

David had been right. The hot tub soothed her churning emotions and left her more relaxed. She'd mixed a few of her salty tears with the chlorinated water and unburdened her heart a little. Mostly she wondered what David had been thinking when he stared at her so long. Short of being a lover's look, it seemed a search for meaning or intent. Maybe he'd doubted the sincerity in her offer to help. Maybe he was looking for truth. Maybe he was looking to see if she felt anything for him. The last one made her stomach flop over. Molly had revealed his thoughts about her. The time wasn't right for that.

But she felt something for him. His kindnesses had stirred a little something inside. Holding her breath, she dunked under the water to wash away what she was thinking. It was too soon to feel something for someone else. It was rebound she was feeling.

Nothing more. But knowing what David was thinking made her nervous. When she'd insisted on helping him, she didn't know how he felt. Now she felt nervous and uncomfortable. The tub suddenly lost its appeal.

Wrinkled and relaxed, she lay on the bed dozing as the snowflakes knocked at the window. Without TV or books to occupy her thoughts, David's list of things to do kept circling in her mind. He needed help. She had two choices. She could sleep away the rest of the day and night away in complete uselessness and boredom in her unhappiness. That way, she wouldn't run the risk of running into Joe or the Colemans. Or she could get up and be helpful on Christmas Eve. Weary travelers would love knowing there was room at the inn. In a way, it was like an unusual version of the Christmas story. And she wanted to be a part of it. This wasn't about her or David or Brandon. It was about an emergency situation. Easy choice.

Viewing herself in the mirror, her chosen outfit, leggings and a Christmas tunic with fleece lined slipper boots, Ashley appeared more cheerful than she felt. After touching up her makeup, she went to find something to do. A cleaning cart was outside her former room. Sounds of scrubbing came from the bathroom. Seeing clean sheets on the dresser, she stripped the beds and piled them onto the cart. She'd started making the beds when David stepped out of the bathroom.

His face immediately turned red and he busied himself with taking off his rubber gloves. "Oh! I didn't know you were here."

Ashley took a deep breath. "Let me give you a hand."

"I can do this. Please, go relax."

She gritted her teeth to try to calm the flare of temper rising inside. "Look. Little girls hear too much and talk too much. Can we agree to ignore what she said? There's too many other things to worry about right now."

With a soft laugh and an easing of his shoulders, he picked the sheets up off the dresser. "Agreed." The red in his face faded a little. "Want to help make beds?"

Two minutes later, they pronounced the room ready and shut the door. Ashley followed David and his cart to the laundry room. As she opened the door, the smell of ammonia hit her nose, making it wrinkle up in response. Shelves of clean sheets and towels lined the back wall, and cleaning supplies sat neatly on shelves across from the washers and dryers.

"I'll wash these sheets later when I have more time."

"I could do it if you like."

David gave her a smile. "That's nice of you to offer, but we should be good if we don't have to change sheets every day or resupply towels. Besides, I want you to enjoy your stay." He nudged her softly to leave the laundry room.

Ashley went out dragging her feet. His consideration of his guests was getting annoying. She needed something to do. Her sanity required it. Anything. A chore to focus her attention away from Brandon. Desperation crept into her voice. "Please, I need to help. I can't stand to sit and do nothing. I need something to fill this...this void. Give me a snow shovel. I'll clear sidewalks."

A look of surprise came across David's face, followed by one that showed he finally got it. "I won't make you work that hard. Linda could use a hand with food preparation, but I can't help her without someone to watch the front desk. Come with me."

As they walked down the corridor, he explained how a semi had jackknifed and closed the interstate. The travelers who hadn't been stopped before the last exit would be directed to come to the lodge until the weather and road conditions improved. So far, an elderly couple named Will and Myra Dugan had come, along with the Mortimer family of four. Three college kids filled one room, Tristan, Cole, and Ed. How many more might come, he didn't know. Six more rooms were available. After that, he'd improvise with cots and sleeping bags.

Stopping at the front desk, David showed her which rooms were empty and how to check people in. Her frequent visits to the lodge left her familiar with pieces of the process, although it felt funny to be on the other side of the desk. Her duties were simple. Greet people as they came in. Show them to their rooms if needed. Keep an eye on the fireplace in the banquet hall and throw on firewood from the overflowing wood box to keep it going so it would warm the banquet hall. If the storm killed the power, people could stay warm in that room. Lastly, keep an eye on Molly. She tended to find mischief when left unattended.

She noticed the white tablecloths and china were gone from the banquet hall, and the tables rearranged into their normal placements. The wedding arch was still there, and the Christmas tree was aglow with hundreds of lights. Otherwise, the large room was lit by only the fire because the heavy drapes across the window blocked out any sunlight showing through the thick snow. The firelight danced across the polished hardwood floor and white walls. The tree's lights added color to the holiday atmosphere. The scene was straight off a Christmas card.

Assuring David she was up to her assigned tasks, she sent him off to the kitchen to consult with Linda on feeding everyone in the banquet hall. She looked around for Molly, but she was nowhere to be found. She'd probably turn up where she least needed to be.

With nothing left to do, she looked in the cabinets behind the desk. Board games, card decks, and extra paperback books sat on the shelves. With people here for the night, the games would get more use if they were set out. Going into the banquet hall, she moved a small table to the side and put decks of cards, several board games, and books for those who might be interested in reading. Old-fashioned entertainment would have to suffice tonight.

The Christmas tree beckoned her with its cheerful look. Colorful packages were stacked around the bottom. Some of them were from her to her family. They'd planned to open gifts after supper tonight, but they probably shouldn't since there weren't gifts for the additional guests. Their gift exchange would have to come at a more appropriate time. In the meantime, she could stash them in her room. Maybe in the morning, she'd invite her family and Uncle Don to her big luxurious room to open Christmas gifts in front of her gas fireplace. Christmas morning would feel more like a normal family gathering.

She stacked the gifts she'd brought, careful not to smash the bows. Most of the boxes had new flannel pajamas meant to be worn tonight for warmth. Everyone would have to enjoy them on Christmas night instead. She made one quick trip to her room and returned for another load.

"Whatcha doing?"

Ashley jerked, grabbing her chest to calm her wildly beating heart. "I didn't see you there!"

Uncle Don leaned around the side of the large chair by the fireplace. A smile wrinkled the skin by his eyes right before he let out a laugh. "Sorry. I was warming myself by the fire. Want to play a game of rummy?"

"Want to help me get these gifts out from under the tree? Since there's not gifts for everyone, I'm taking the ones I brought to my room so they don't get lost or accidently opened by mischievous hands."

With a soft grunt, Uncle Don lifted himself out of the cushy chair. "Sure, I'll help." He came over and held his arms out for loading.

She stacked several of the gifts before handing them to him. As she helped him get a good hold on them, she caught a movement out of the corner of her eye. Looking around, she saw a pair of blue eyes surrounded by blonde hair peeking around a chair. Molly was still slinking around and spying on people. She'd probably seen more than her daddy ever knew. Now she had an accomplice. Behind her were a pair of brown eyes underneath black bangs.

Maybe the other girl was from the family David said had arrived. Molly was teaching her bad habits.

Being watched was no problem. She wasn't doing anything that would cause tongues to wag or doing anything embarrassing to anyone. As long as no blackmail was involved, she was safe.

Stacking up the last of her gifts, she stood up and turned. Uncle Don's warning came too late, and she almost tripped over Molly and her friend who stood right behind her. The gifts were tossed slightly into the air, and Ashley juggled hard to keep any from falling. Regaining her balance, she shouted, "Molly!" Her breath came hard with her racing heart. "Don't do that! You shouldn't sneak up behind people."

Molly narrowed her eyes, looking from one thief to the other. "Are you stealing from Santa?"

The other girl stood behind Molly, wide-eyed and taking everything in.

A giggle escaped Ashley's lips. "No. Santa didn't bring these. I did. I'm taking them out from under the tree so that my gifts don't get mixed up with the ones Santa is bringing tonight."

Molly cocked her head. "Are you sure? Santa knows when you've been naughty. I heard you yelling at your mother, and Daddy says that's naughty!"

Ashley took a step back. "You were listening through the door?" A smug look on the girl's face affirmed her suspicion. "Spying on people is naughty too. Santa won't be visiting you tonight either."

With a humpf, Molly slapped her hands on her hips. "Yes, he will! Daddy said so."

Leaning down to her level, Uncle Don whispered, "Does your daddy know that you listen at people's doors without them knowing?"

Slowly, Molly's hands hung at her side as she looked at the floor and ran the toe of her slipper along a seam of wood in the floor. Guilt had no hiding place.

Uncle Don stood up. "Hum, I thought not. You need to stop doing that. It's rude and it's naughty."

Adding her concurrence, Ashley nodded. Turning her attention to the wide-eyed girl watching them, she asked, "Who's your friend?"

Molly's confident look bounced back. She turned and pulled her friend closer to Ashley. "Her name's Keisha. Her family got stuck in the snow, so they had to come here. She's sad because Santa thinks she'll be at her grandparents' house in Denver." She pointed at Ashley. "This lady is a princess named Ashley. She gave me her crown."

Ashley put the gifts onto one arm and took Keisha's hand. "Nice to meet you. You don't need to worry. Santa has magic. I bet he'll find you here. Maybe he'll leave some presents here for you and more at your grandparents' house. Wouldn't that be fun? Presents at two houses!"

Keisha looked puzzled at first, but slowly a light came into her eyes. "Wow! That would be cool!" She jumped up and down with a smile spread wide by her joy.

Molly didn't seem as enthusiastic as her friend. A not-fair sentiment was plainly showing on her face and was probably ready to explode out of her mouth. Time to change the subject.

"Could you two be good girls and help me out? Go stand by the front desk and watch for people wanting a room. If anyone comes, please tell them I'll be right back to check them in."

Molly perked up. "Daddy lets me do that sometimes. It's an important job."

"Good! You know how to do it then. I'll be right back." Seeing the girls skip off to the front desk holding hands, Ashley and Uncle Don hurried to her room with the last load.

While she stashed the gifts in the closet, he asked, "How are you feeling? You seem calm and normal, like nothing has happened. Have you cried to let it all out? Or are you stifling your true feelings to make sure everyone else has a good time?"

She stood and rubbed the slight cramp in her lower back. "I've cried. I've mostly accepted that Brandon is gone, and I've lost my oldest girlfriend. I don't know what to do now. How do I start over when they were so intertwined with my life?"

His strong arms embraced her and held her close. The aroma of Old Spice transformed her into the little girl he used to hug that way when she was crying with a skinned knee. "I felt that way when I lost your Aunt Marge. I felt very lost and alone. I did what I had to do. Take one step at a time. One day at a time. You'll do that and make a new path for yourself."

With her face buried in his shoulder, she nodded.

"Now, wipe your eyes and let's go see what trouble those two girls have found."

Pulling away, she murmured as she found her brush and ran it through her hair, "Those girls! Can you imagine what Molly's seen and heard around here?" Her hand froze as a thought came and stuck. "I wonder if she saw or heard anything from Jessica or Brandon?" She stared at Uncle Don whose eyes were wide.

"I wonder too."

Pacing, she wondered aloud, "But how do you ask a little girl what's she's seen or heard while spying? I'd need to get permission from her dad to grill the little spy. Of course, I wouldn't call her that in front of him."

"Of course not."

Stopping in front of her uncle, she asked him, "What should I do?"

He lifted one shoulder. "You can do what you want, but if it were me, I'd wait for an opening. The girl may eventually spill the beans and you won't have to ask. Or Brandon may show up, and you can ask him all of your questions."

Indecision anchored her to the spot. He was telling her to be patient. That wasn't something she wanted to do. She wanted to grab Molly by the shoulders and demand to know what she'd seen and heard in the last 24 hours, but David would be furious. She didn't dare lose his respect. He'd been very good to her.

Uncle Don waved his hand in front of Ashley's face. "Wake up. Remember. Those girls are unsupervised."

A bolt of fear jerked her into action. While she applied lipstick, Uncle Don went back to his room. She rushed back to the lobby where things seemed peaceful. True to her word, Molly stood guard there, telling Keisha how things were done.

Not wanting to entertain the girls, she handed them a card deck of the Match Game and sent them off to the banquet hall. She'd keep an eye on them in there while she tried to figure out something to put under the tree for Keisha. She'd promised Santa's magic to work, and she was the elf to make it happen.

CHAPTER 5

· ▾ · ▾ · ♠ · ▾ · ▾ ·

I n the back entrance to the inn, David and Brett put on their snow boots and heavy coats. Blowing snow and drifts lay between them and the storage shed out back which held their emergency supplies. Neither man had thought to bring in the kerosene lanterns or cots before the storm hit. The bite of the cold would make them pay for their lack of foresight.

Brett picked up a cotton rope. "Let's tie this to the back door and make our way to the shed. Then we'll follow the rope back here. I don't want the wind to blow us off course so bad we miss getting back inside."

"I would have never thought to do it," David said as he pulled his woolen hat over his ears. "Ready?" he asked through the scarf around his face.

Brett nodded, and David opened the door. The snow rushed inside, filling the room like it was a shaken snow globe. Brett tied the rope to the door handle and took a step out. Grabbing the crook of Brett's arm in one hand and the rope handle of the small wood sled with the other, David started toward the shed. The strong wind pushed them to the side, making their trek hard and staying on course harder. The snow was nearly up to their knees.

Much deeper and they'd need snowshoes to get out there again. Gradually, they could see the outline of the shed through the snow and changed direction to get them to their destination.

Their next challenge was unlocking the padlock that protected the shed's contents. If he pulled his glove off, David knew his hand would freeze within a minute. Yet, if he didn't take his gloves off, he might drop the key in the snow and they'd probably never find it until spring. Turning his back to the wind, he slipped off his glove and felt inside his coat pocket for the key ring. Finding it, he quickly unlocked the padlock and immediately put his hand in his pocket. His finger stung a little from the cold but having access to supplies was worth it.

Pulling the sled inside, David helped Brett tie the rope to the lodge to the sled. They both pushed on the door to keep the storm from following them in. The men stomped the snow off their feet and blew warm breaths into their ungloved hands. A flip of the switch and light filled the small shed, revealing the rows of shelves with neatly organized supplies for running the lodge.

"Those kerosene lanterns are in the back," Brett said, his words vaporizing from his mouth. "The battery-operated ones are on the other side."

"I hope we have enough," David said as he started that way. The lights flickered, halting him in his tracks. "That's not good."

"I hope we have enough batteries and kerosene to last until the roads open. Long nights and short tempers make for an uncomfortable mixture."

"Especially with that Joe guy. An alcoholic on the prowl is dangerous." David opened a box and looked inside. Not finding what he wanted, he went on to the next one. "Other people may join him in his hunt as they come in. Ashley specifically asked that no alcohol be served while she was here. Her Uncle Don used to drink too much. He's been sober for years, but she didn't want it tempting anyone. My agreement with her is coming back on me, not her. Our other guests may demand to be served."

"Here's the lanterns and batteries," Brett said as he pulled a box from the shelf and carried it to the sled. "The kerosene lanterns are here too." He set two large cans on the sled. "Don't worry about serving beer. If it gets out of hand, you can always ask her to let you out of that part of the contract. IF she says no, we'll find some way to handle it. One thing at a time."

Pulling out three boxes, they carried them to the door and put them on the sled.

The threat of darkness had been somewhat conquered. One battery lantern to a room would allow guests to see well enough to get ready for bed but wouldn't allow reading a book very long. It would have to do. People would need to spend most of their time in the banquet hall where the brighter and longer lasting kerosene lanterns would be. Even if his customers wouldn't be pleased with going to bed with the sun, at least they'd find their way around.

Running the generator would keep the food supplies cooled and run the stove and microwave so they could be served. The water pump on the well would keep working so they could use bathrooms and clean the kitchen. The generator wouldn't support heating all the individual rooms. They'd turn the breakers off in the places they could and run the heat to a few rooms during the night only. The alternative would be sleeping on cots in the banquet hall with the fireplace. No one would like that, least of all him. Tension squeezed David's chest. He breathed deeply to loosen its grip, but it remained tight.

"As long as we're here," Brett said as he went to the other side of the shelving, "we may as well take in these cots and sleeping bags. You know, the ones we got when we talked about setting up several tepees, but never did."

The memory forced a small smile on David's face. Monica thought they could draw customers by letting people sleep in tepees in the woods behind the lodge. The grand experiment lasted one summer. The tepees couldn't compete with the comfortable beds near the bathrooms in the lodge. Few guests requested the primitive accommodations, and the idea was quickly abandoned. One of the rare bumps in Monica's excellent business dealings.

David helped Brett pull the boxes of cots and sleeping bags off the top shelf. "I never thought we'd use these again. Good thing we didn't haul them to the dump like we talked about."

The two men tied down the cots, sleeping bags, the kerosene lanterns, kerosene, battery lights, and batteries on the sled. The tension eased a little in David as he counted his supplies. If the generator couldn't heat the lodge, they had enough cots for everyone to sleep in front of the fireplace provided no one else came. If worse came to worse, they'd drag mattresses from the rooms into the banquet hall. This improvisation would likely be for only one night. Last time he saw the weather forecast, the storm would probably be gone by morning. His guests might get to go home by mid-afternoon after the highways were cleared. He would hope and pray for that.

They loaded more blankets and pillows on the sled before covering the load with a tarp and tying it down again. Pulling their heavy coats on, they wrapped up to go back into the storm. With a nod to each other, they opened the door and started out. Even though it was late afternoon, the thick clouds made it seem like dusk. Their tracks through the deep snow were almost filled in so they had to break a new trail. The sled was heavy and sank into the deep snow. The trip going back required one man pushing and one man pulling. Following the rope back to the lodge, they made their way, moving snow before pulling the heavy sled. After much effort, they reached the area under the overhang where the snow wasn't as deep.

Opening the back door, David went in and took their goods from Brett as he unloaded them. Brett stashed the sled against the wall and followed David into the warm room. Stomping their feet and shedding their outer layers, they congratulated each other on a successful mission.

Linda came into the back room and looked at the pile of boxes and remarked, "Oh good, you remembered the cots. State Patrol brought two semi drivers and a family of three named Smith. After that, they will be pulling in. It's too dangerous for them to be out there. If they hear from anyone else, it'll be up to search and rescue to decide whether to make a try for them or not."

Brett paused in his celebration of being indoors for the rest of the storm. "Search and rescue?"

Linda nodded as she crossed her arms. "You heard it right. So keep your Paks warm, Brett. It may be a long night. As soon as the snow lets up, we may need the snowmobiles."

David froze. Brett and Linda ran the local search-and-rescue team. They occasionally left their duties at the lodge to go help someone in need, and his other employees filled in the giant holes left behind when they were gone. But tonight, he had no other employees to fill in behind them if they were called out. How could he take care of all these people at the lodge by himself? Even feeding them all required all three of them.

As if reading his mind, Linda added, "We'll make food up tonight, then if we get called out, it shouldn't be too much trouble for you to feed everyone. Some of them may even pitch in to help."

An arm went around David's shoulders before Brett's deep voice filled his hear. "See, boss, you got nothing to worry about." He gave a hearty laugh as he went inside with Linda.

Hanging up his heavy coat on a hook, David's stress boiled over. His to-do list had just mushroomed.

The smell of cooking meat, herbs, and bread filled the lodge's kitchen. A large pot of beef stew simmered on the stove, part of tonight's supper. While Linda took a large pan of rolls out of the oven, Brett stood over a frying pan tending to the cooking chicken breasts. Next to him, David pulled and diced the cooked chicken before dumping it into a large bowl. Serving chicken salad sandwiches not only spread their resources farther but required no heat before serving. Keeping it cool was no problem. If the electricity went out, they'd put it outside in the snowbank.

A lantern burned on the cabinet in case the lights went out. With so many sharp instruments and hot surfaces in use, dark was an enemy to fingers. Kerosene lanterns were strategically placed on the reception desk and in the banquet hall with signs on them stating authorized personal would light them in case of a power outage. Each guest was issued a battery lantern for use in their rooms. Part of their emergency plan was in place.

From the corner of his eye, David saw Ashley slicing vegetables. The force of her knife cutting through carrots seemed slightly excessive, probably fueled by visions of her ex. Her lips moved slightly as she carried on a conversation with an unseen person. She grabbed an onion and with a mighty whack and a smirk on her face, cut it in half. When she finally put the knife down, the onion was finely minced.

The violence in his kitchen made him nervous. Butchering vegetables might be therapy for her broken heart, but he'd keep an eye on the knife just in case she decided more than vegetables needed to die.

He refocused on his chicken shredding until a loud thud drew everyone's eyes to Ashley. Tomato halves lay on either side of the cutting board that had a knife fixed in it. Ashley glared at the two halves. Working the knife out of the cutting board, she picked up another one and whacked it in half, embedding the knife again. Her hand reached again, evidently not intending to stop until she'd taken her anger out on all the innocent tomatoes.

David exchanged glances with Linda and Brett. Waving the men toward the door, Linda grabbed a head of lettuce and gave it to Ashley. "Here, sweetie, think of this as your absent groom."

The loud whack that followed sent David and Brett beating it out of the man-hating atmosphere. As they rounded the corner of the banquet hall, the lights went off, stopping the men in their tracks as their eyes adjusted to the firelight. Cries for Daddy rang out from the dark corner of the room.

David called out to the girls to follow his voice which silenced Molly's and Keisha's cries for help. Emergency lights lit the hallway but would only last an hour. When the girls found him, he led them out to the lobby that was lit by the dim afternoon sun through the long, narrow windows beside the door, leaving Brett to light the kerosene lanterns.

Down the hallway, people popped out of their rooms, yelling and asking what was going on. David told everyone to get their battery lanterns and come to the banquet hall. They'd discuss the plans for the night there. Keisha skittered off to her parents when they called her name.

The banquet hall took on a quaint glow by the light of the kerosene lanterns, accented by the glow of cell phones. Brett adjusted and repositioned the lanterns to get the maximum light from them. People milled around in front of the fireplace, all talking at the same time. The wedding guests and the refugees from the storm stood apart from each other. Like oil and water, no one wanted to mix with the other side.

Raising his hands to ask for silence, David tried to calm everyone. "There's no reason to panic. The power is off, but we've made provisions to keep everyone warm and fed. I suggest you send a few text messages to let your families know you're safe, then turn off your cell phones. Without power, there'll be no recharging if you run your batteries down. Please sit down. I'll tell you our plan for this evening and tonight."

The mumblers and grumblers filled the seats at the tables as hostility filled the air. No one was where they expected to be on Christmas Eve. The holiday was ruined, and everyone seemed determined to find someone to blame. Their questions hovered in the air like a swarm of gnats circling heads and looking for things to annoy.

"Don't you have a generator?"

"My phone is almost dead! I need a charge!"

"I'm cold. When can we leave?"

"Have you called the power company? Will they send someone out?"

"I don't like my room. Have anything else?"

"Where's the booze? I need a drink!"

"I have to use the bathroom."

"What are you doing to find my son? He's out there in the storm, maybe dying. Go find him!"

The grief-stricken face of Rhonda stood out from everyone else. Bob held her close as her eyes filled with tears.

David could understand her agony, not knowing where her son was. At the same time, Brandon had chosen his course of action. Let the young man and the girl play the hand they dealt to themselves. He looked away, unsettled by his lack of compassion, but he had to think of all his guests.

"Brandon's probably in a hotel room somewhere so shut up about it!"

Maggie's outburst and Rhonda's cry of anger drew everyone's quiet attention to them. Both started to rise, but their husbands pushed them back down into the chairs. Behind Bob, Joe's bored looked suddenly turned to amusement and impishness.

Spinning around, David threw another log on the fire to buy time. His throat was tight. He clinched his jaw to hold the harsh words from spilling out of his mouth. He'd love to lock both women in their rooms.

Brett came up beside him and patted him on the shoulder. "Time to regain control."

Taking a deep breath in, he let it out slowly before turning to face his guests. He had a kitchen with an armed vegetable-whacker, two women itching for a fight, a room full of unhappy guests, no staff, Brett and Linda possible going out on search-and rescue trips. He was one man in this sea of confusion. Somehow, he had to find a way to assure them they were safe, electricity or no. They had food, fire, and shelter, the basics of life. With a storm like the one raging outside, they were lucky to be here.

The murmuring grew in volume as more people asked questions about the two women who continued to glare at each other in a fury as hot as the sun. Some asked her what Rhonda was talking about and Bob explained the whole sordid mess to them. As he answered their questions, his finger occasionally waved toward Maggie and Randy. Hostility started drifting in the room like the scent of a freshly lit scented candle. Lines were being drawn in the floor, and guests were choosing sides between the mother of the former bride and the mother of the former groom. When he saw their lips starting to move, he knew trouble was coming fast and furious.

David felt another poke in his back. Brett reminded him it was time to regain control, like he couldn't figure that out himself. Coughing and clearing his throat so he could use his I'm-the-boss voice, David said, "Ladies and gentlemen, I need your attention!"

The din of the conversations drowned out his voice except for the ones closest to him. Two truckers standing near him gave him a sideways look of boredom and turned their attention back to the more exciting argument between the wedding party mothers that was growing louder.

From the sound of the crowd, time to regain control had come and gone. It was now time to intervene before a brawl started.

People began to get out of their seats. They formed battle lines on each side, then closed ranks to form an arena in the middle. He could see between the two truckers standing beside each other as they watched the unfolding drama. Joe circled the outer perimeter of the circle, whispering something.

Maggie broke free of Randy and went to get into the face of Rhonda who met her in the middle of the war zone. "You're son is a no-count, low-life bum who left my daughter at the altar! He deserves to be miserable out in the storm."

And thus the first shot was fired.

"Excuse me," David said to the tall trucker in front of him. Getting no response to his request, he stuck his arm between them like a pry bar and tried to slip past them. "Excuse me," he said again. He didn't look at them but felt the heat of their glares as he pushed past the two large men.

Rhonda shoved Bob away from her and got into Maggie's face. "Your daughter ran him off! If he dies out there in the storm, I'll sue her for wrongful death!"

Joe started a low chanting that started spreading. "Fight. Fight. Fight."

Randy pushed Maggie to the side and pointed his finger in Rhonda's face. "Don't threaten our daughter. She did nothing wrong." His face grew redder as his eyebrows lowered. "Brandon made the choice to leave. He didn't have enough brains to see that it was a stupid decision. And he's risking Jessica's life by luring her to go with him."

"Fight. Fight. Fight." Joe continued to chant as he circled the crowd. The chant grew a little louder but quieted as Bob came around Rhonda and chest-bumped Randy.

David pushed past spellbound children on the edge of the arena. Putting an arm and shoulder between the combatants, he said in the calmest voice he could manage, "Now, people, let's—"

With a loud growl, Maggie lunged at Rhonda. Her fingers grabbed a handful of hair and pulled. Rhonda howled and scratched at her assailant with claws drawn but hit David's side. Her manicured nails ripped his flannel shirt with a loud rip. Three red lines could be seen on his skin as he yelped in pain. The sound stunned the women enough that their husbands had the briefest of seconds to grab them.

David put his hand over his exposed skin.

"Daddy!" Molly screamed at the top of her vocal range. "You hurt my Daddy!" Tears and sobs followed her scream. She ran and grabbed him around the waist.

Pulling his daughter to one side of the arena, he sheltered her from the feuding couples. His face was hot, matching his insides. No one could upset his daughter without answering to him. "Look what your fighting has done! You're scaring the kids." He left Molly in Brett's hands and stepped into the small space between the couples. "Plus you're upsetting my guests. Take this fight out in the snowbank if you—"

Rhonda was focused on the Chens, like a lion about to move in on its prey. She stepped around David like he wasn't there and screamed at the Chens, "Ashley never loved him! Why isn't she out there looking for him if she really loved him?" She took a step back as her face contorted into a grimace that she quickly controlled. "Has she cried one tear? Has she shown any heartache at him leaving? No! She's made of ice. No wonder he left."

A voice of anger rang out from behind the circled crowd. "What is going on here?"

With a glare that would melt steel, Ashley stepped into the circle and stared at each of the combatants. "I asked you all a question. Are you sharing our dirty laundry with everyone?"

David stepped back to join Molly, Brett, and Linda, afraid of the hot anger emitting from the young woman. The fury of this scorned woman was directed at the four parents in the middle of the circle. Best to stay far away from the explosion.

"What did I miss?" Linda whispered to Brett.

"Round one," he whispered back.

With arms spread wide, Ashley turned in a circle, addressing the crowd. "Let me finish this for everyone's benefit. This was supposed to be my wedding day, but the groom ran off with the maid of..." she choked a little. "You get the idea," she murmured.

A collective ooohhh wafted from the circled crowd.

"Now my parents and the parents of the absent groom are facing off like a bunch of hillbillies, embarrassing me and them. Since they are acting like children, I will declare a truce between the sides..." she glared at the four parents, "...and there will be no more fighting. And Joe, shut your stupid fat mouth."

The man's mouth flew open. "What did I do?"

"Quit acting dumb. Oh, sorry. I know you can't help it." Ashley put her hands on her hips and lowered her head as she took a deep breath.

The suddenly meek Maggie put her arms around her daughter's shoulders. "The Colemans were saying terrible things about you. Of course, your father and I had to defend you." A weak smile crossed her face.

Ashley pushed her mother away. "You acted shamefully."

Rhonda shook her finger at Ashley. "Because of you, Brandon may be freezing to death in a snowbank." Tears filled her eyes.

"Aren't you worried about him even a little? I thought you loved him."

David and the crowd turned to Ashley, watching her face as it flickered between anger and anguish. Like a ball on a roulette table, he wondered where her emotions would land. Most women who'd been through what she'd been through this day would have crumbled and cried all day long. But he'd caught a glimpse of her inner feelings when he helped her move her things into the honeymoon suite. Her broken heart was there inside her, held in check by her self-control.

Ashley bit her lip. "Of course I loved him, but he betrayed me. He cheated on me. I find it hard to love him now. Any tears I cry are for me and the death of my dream."

A sniff came from behind David, and a woman across from him was blinking her eyes far more than normal. Calm had been restored by the one who was feeling it the least. A tingling started in his heart, one he hadn't felt in a long time. This woman had sparked something inside him. He'd felt guilty for feeling an attraction for her, but no more. He admired her for her strength. His heart went out to her as she stared at her feet.

Joe let out a low laugh. His lip curled as he said, "Boo hoo for you. Enough of this pity party. Bring out the booze."

A bolt of fight flashed through David. Punching the guy in the mouth would ease that feeling. Randy must have had the same thought as he took a step toward Joe.

"Don't be such an insensitive jerk, man," one of the truckers said. "A broken heart is not trivial."

Pulling his pants up by his belt, Joe faced off with the trucker who stood a head taller and looked like he might have played for the NFL at some point in time. The lopsided matchup was cut short when several other people stepped behind the trucker. Joe's eyes scanned all his opponents as his face reddened. He stepped back and shrugged. "Whatever," he mumbled.

An unsteady truce had been reached. Relieved, David stepped to the center of the crowd to keep them there for a little longer. To douse the flames, he switched the topic from something inflammatory to something important to them all. He explained how they would deal with the situation. Cots would be set up in the banquet hall for anyone who wanted to stay warm by the fire, but they were welcome to stay in their rooms too. Extra blankets, food, and water would be provided, but no alcohol.

The last item elicited a loud protest from Joe and others. The arguments got louder and more intense as he kept shaking his head.

The long day was weighing heavy on David's shoulders, bringing with it a dull headache that was spreading. Adding alcohol to this volatile crowd would be a mistake. The sooner he got everyone fed and to bed, the easier peace would be maintained.

Out of the corner of his eye, he saw Don walk up to Ashley. Something he whispered in her ear that made her head bob up and down and a smile spread across her face. She wiped her face and moved like she was throwing off a heavy blanket from her shoulders. "It's Christmas Eve, everybody! Time to put hard feelings aside. Time for peace and good will toward everyone."

Quiet dulled the bickering. People listened to the woman in the middle.

Ashley turned around slowly, eyeing all the circled crowd. "Thanks to our innkeeper David…" she waved her arm toward him, "…we're all safe and warm here, out of the storm. We have a nice meal planned. Think of that night long ago when there was no room at the inn for tired travelers. Good things came to bless all of mankind. We have a Christmas tree. Let's celebrate the season!"

People stood silent and unmoving as the fireplace crackled and popped. A few of the phone screens blacked out. Softly, very low, humming started. The sound gradually grew a little louder and a little louder until someone started singing the words. "Silent night, holy night…"

David felt the warm hand of his daughter slip into his. He gave it a squeeze as his chin trembled slightly. The one who had the most to complain about had lifted everyone else's spirits. Including his. All his doubt was wiped away. He was falling in love.

CHAPTER 6

·▾·▾·♥·▾·▾·

As the snow fell, hot chocolate and eggnog warmed and fueled the board and card games in the banquet hall. One of the truckers passed out candy canes to the children. The large pot of beef stew and warm rolls disappeared quickly, with leftover wedding cake for dessert. Christmas carols sung by a group in front of the tree provided music for everyone. The Christmas spirit was alive and well in most corners of Spruce Canyon Lodge, much to Ashley's delight.

Boredom over his fate had vanished from Mason. When the Mortimers arrived, they brought their attractive teenaged daughter Emily, who looked to be about Mason's age. The distance between them quickly shrank and now, they couldn't seem to sit close enough or get in places dark enough. Like a watch dog, Stanley Mortimer, Emily's dad, kept a close eye on both of them.

One cheerless spot remained. Randy and Maggie sat at a table on one side of the fireplace, whispering to each other a little, but mostly staring at the fire. One the other side of the fireplace, Bob and Rhonda sat silently, still as statues, leaning against each other. An occasional wipe of the face with a tissue hinted that they were still alive. Between the two couples sat Uncle Don, reading a book by firelight and ensuring the peace was kept.

Absent from the room was Joe. Ashley wondered where he was, but really didn't care as long as he wasn't stirring up trouble. The ambience was more peaceful without him around.

An alarm on a cell phone interrupted the festive scene, and a parent declared it was time for good children to be in bed with promises that Santa Claus would find them. With groans and excited yells, children were ferried off to their rooms to get ready for bed. Most of the adults called it a night and debated on whether to sleep in their chilly rooms or sleep on a cot in the banquet hall. While the children were getting their pajamas on, a few men made quick forays to the cars to retrieve gifts and stashed them behind the reception desk. A designated elf would put them under the tree when the children were all asleep.

Ashley tried to keep Molly preoccupied so she wouldn't see the Santas bring in gifts from the cars. She skipped back and forth in front of the decorated tree, singing Christmas songs at the top of her lungs. Ashley wondered where David had gone, but he was nowhere to be seen. Trying to quiet the girl was almost impossible until she reminded her keeping others awake would reflect badly on her good-girl status. She settled down on the sofa in front of the fireplace where Ashley read a book to her.

The personification of Mrs. Claus, otherwise known as Myra Dugan, walked into the banquet hall. Her thick, red bathrobe and dark fuzzy slippers were topped with a Santa hat over her gray hair. Looking pleased with herself, she sauntered to the sofa and announced, "Will and I decided we'd rather be warm than comfortable, so we'll be staking out a couple of cots."

For an instant, Molly sat still, wide-eyed with wonder. With one bounce, Molly was off the sofa and standing in front of Myra. "We call it camping, when me and Daddy stay in here. Sometimes we roast marshmallows too. It's so fun."

"Don't you have a nice daddy," Myra said with a smile in her voice, touching Molly's chin. "I take it your mother isn't here. Where does she live?"

Leaning against the arm of the sofa, she replied, "In Heaven. Daddy says she watches over us, and she can see us camping."

Myra's fingers went to her mouth to stop a mournful gasp. Reaching out, she gathered the girl into her arms and planted a kiss on the cheek. "Bless you child. And bless your sweet daddy." She turned to Ashley and said, "And bless you for the hard day you've had."

Dismissing the sympathy with a shrug and a half smile, Ashley murmured her thanks.

Reflecting his wife's apparel, Will came in with his Santa hat slightly askew, his arms full of pillows and blankets for their cots. With a Merry Christmas and good night, the pair made their way to a dark corner of the room where two cots waited for them.

Stanley came around the corner to stand beside the fireplace as he warmed himself after his foray to his car. "It's still snowing but not as hard. If the wind would die down, I'd have a little hope that the storm may be gone by morning."

Ashley nodded. "That's good news. One night without electricity is an adventure. Anything beyond that is hardship."

With a small laugh, he bid her a good night.

The burned wood in the fireplace shifted, sending a few sparks up and out. Molly rushed to sweep the embers back toward the hearth as Ashley added more wood. Satisfied with the increasing flames, Ashley took Molly's hand. "Come on, let's go find your dad. It's past your bedtime." They were about to go into the kitchen when the doors to the lodge flew open. Snow swirled around three figures in the doorway. A woman in the middle slumped against a man on one side while a state patrol officer held her arm on the other side. She stood behind a very large belly. A groan came from her lips as they stumbled inside.

"We need help!" the man who held her cried out as he helped her toward the reception counter. They took two steps when a flood of liquid splattered all over the floor beneath the woman.

From behind Ashley came Molly's voice. "She peed all over the floor! Dad will be maaaddd!"

Functioning on adrenaline more than good sense, Ashley yelled, "Molly, go find your dad! Quick!" She waved the men toward the hallway. Rushing behind the reception desk, she grabbed the key with the lowest number on it and her lantern before leading them to the first available room. Throwing the door open, she told them, "Lay her down on this first bed. I'll get towels and more sheets."

She ran to the laundry room, her mind full of imaginations of what was going to happen. She'd never had a baby or even seen one born except in movies or on TV. But her mother had. She grabbed the phone and dialed her parents' room. Explaining the situation, she asked her mother to come help. "And get Rhonda. She used to work in a doctor's office. Maybe she knows a little."

Her mother sputtered, "I can't help! I don't remember much from when I had you and your brother. And Rhonda. She worked in a podiatrist office. Unless the woman has an ingrown toenail, she's probably no use either."

"Get her anyway. Maybe she can help do something."

Not waiting for an answer, she hung up and gathered an armful of towels and sheets and hurried back to the room. The patrolman paced outside the door. The woman was groaning and yelling at her husband and calling for her doctor as Ashley went in. A man held the woman's hand and told her they couldn't get to the hospital which made her scream something at him that hurt Ashley's ears.

David stood against the wall, white-faced and worried. Linda came running into the room. Taking control, she instructed David to get some whiskey and scissors.

"Okay," he said as he rushed away. "I'll turn the heat on in this room."

Bending over the prostrate woman, Linda asked, "What's your name, sweetie?"

The man she clung to answered for her. "Her name's Jenna. I'm her husband Adam. We were on the way to the hospital when we ran off the road. If it hadn't been for this patrolman, we'd still be out there." A look of sheer panic twisted his face and his hands shook like they were about to jump off his arms.

Linda grabbed him by the wrist. "You're fine. I'm an EMT. I can help you with your baby so relax. Everything is under control. You need to stay calm for Jenna's sake. Why don't you get these wet clothes off her."

As her husband disrobed his wife in between contractions, Linda pointed at Ashley. "Good. You brought sheets and towels. Help me with them." She flung back the comforter back on the other bed. She took all the towels Ashley brought and spread them out on one side of the bed. Taking a sheet, she folded it into quarters and lay it over the towels. She took another sheet and repeated the action. "Go get more towels," she commanded Ashley.

Relieved at being told what to do, Ashley hurried back to the laundry room. Linda knew what she was doing which was a huge relief. Someone else could make the decisions. Watching the front desk and cutting up produce was not a problem, but delivering a baby? No way! Just the thought of it made her cringe inside. She and Brandon had talked of having children, but the sight of that distraught woman calling her husband ugly names, the smell of blood, and the sounds of pain had changed her mind.

David's voice brought her out of her soul-searching. "Linda's asking if you got those towels?"

Handing him her armful, she grabbed more sheets and blankets before following him back down the hallway. They'd moved the woman to the bed that had been prepared for her. Her bare legs and lower torso were exposed. Her husband leaned over her, holding her shoulders while telling her how to breathe. The fierce look in her eyes was unmistakable. She blamed him for what was happening and would kill him as soon as she was able.

Ashley couldn't take her eyes off the sweating woman who held her bulbous belly while she moaned. She had to stare. She'd never seen such a sight, and it left her frozen. She felt David take the towels out of her arms, then took her arm and pulled her out of the room. She couldn't help herself. She must have looked stunned because when they were outside the room, David asked if she was okay.

"I've just never—" She was interrupted when her mother and Rhonda came rushing toward her. A temporary truce seemed to be in place. "I mean—" The words weren't there to speak.

Her mother wore the jeans and a sweatshirt she'd worn driving to the lodge. She stated in a no-nonsense voice, "We're here, although I'm not sure we'll be much help."

Rhonda grabbed Ashley's arm. "How is the woman doing?"

As if in response to the question, a loud, R-rated yell came from behind the closed door.

The four of them stood staring at the closed door until David said, "She's in good hands. Linda knows what she's doing. If you'll excuse me, I need to find out what Molly's up to. She probably has questions, and it's way past her bedtime."

The three women went to the lobby where Brett was cleaning the floor. The patrolman who'd brought the pregnant lady in was sipping a mug of something warm while he watched. The sound of voices drifted around the corner of the banquet hall. Sleep would have to wait until the excitement died down.

Rhonda rushed to the patrolman. "Sir, have you seen my son? He left here sometime very early this morning. He's driving a white Honda CRV." She let out an agonized groan and wrung her hands. "I told him to buy the red one, but he wouldn't listen to me. He might be lost out there, but no one will find him in that white thing he drives, and he'll freeze to death!" She broke down and started crying.

The patrolman reached out to her and pulled her into a supportive hug. Ashley offered her a tissue from behind the reception desk. She continued to sob so Ashley handed her the box.

"Don't worry, ma'am," the patrolman said. "If he stays with his vehicle, he should be fine. I've been ordered to stay here because the road is closed. Any vehicles out on the road will have to wait until morning. The search and rescue teams will be out as soon as the storm lets up and the plows go out." He patted her back a couple of times and gave Ashley and Maggie a look that said "help!"

Ashley pulled on the sniffling woman. "Come on, Rhonda, he'll be fine. Come sit by the fire where it's warm. Search-and-rescue will find him and Jessica as soon as they can." With her arm around her, she guided the woman to the sofa in front of the fireplace. She whispered to her mother, "Go get Bob." Maggie hurried away.

The patrolman followed them in and backed up in front of the fire. "My name's Jim. I'm on the rescue team along with Brett here, and we'll be out looking for anyone stranded in the storm as soon as we can. We have snowmobiles, so we can handle deep snow. It being Christmas Eve and all, there may be lots of people out there.

I hope not, but we'll get to them as fast as we can when we can do so safely."

A hard gust of wind whistled down the chimney and rattled the front door. The two truckers, Joe, Cole, and Tristan played poker in the corner. They stopped and looked at the people gathering in front of the fire.

"If people stay in their cars, they'll be fine," Brett murmured as the hurricane of frozen water beat against the windows. Without another word, he went back to his work in the lobby. The sound of his squeezing the water out of the mop before he plopped it on the floor drifted into the banquet room.

Rhonda drew a ragged breath, followed by a slight hiccup. "Brandon isn't known for being intelligent. The smartest thing he ever did was fall in love with Ashley. And he didn't do that right either." Her sobbing kicked up and she lay face down on the sofa.

The poker game broke up, along with the other conversations. Everyone but Joe left the room, leaving Ashley with the crying woman.

Ashley wondered what she should do to keep Rhonda's tears and snot from marring the beautiful leather sofa. Grabbing a hand full of tissues, she pushed them on the side of her face. Where was Bob? Surely her mother was there by now.

As if hearing her prayer, Bob appeared and pulled his wife off the sofa. "Come now, dear," he said as she folded herself onto him like a limp rag. "It's time for bed." He put his arm under hers and dragged her away, leaving the others to stare after them.

A sly grin covered Joe's face as he quickly slid into the spot left vacant by Rhonda. "How ya doing?" he said in a voice dripping in sugary sap.

Her mood left her unwilling to listen to much. "What do you want, Joe."

Scratching the side of his neck, he confessed, "That game of poker wasn't my best. The cards were against me. Seems I'm out more money than I brought with me. So how 'bout it? Can you float me a loan?"

Curiosity drove her to ask the question, "How much?"

"A couple hundred."

A laugh bubbled out of her. The forlorn look on Joe's face made her laugh harder.

Joe stood up. "Does that mean you're not going to help me? What do you suggest I do?"

Biting her lips together to stop her levity, she finally said, "I suggest you promise to dig their trucks out of the snow tomorrow morning. Sorry, Joe, you got yourself into this. Get yourself out."

A flurry of curse words flew from him, but he was swiftly reprimanded by Brett. In a huff, he stormed down the hallway.

"Thanks, Brett," Ashley said as she settled back on the sofa.

"He's harmless. Just dumb as a post." Scratching his thick brown hair, Brett leaned against the mop handle. "That poor Rhonda woman. I can understand why she's upset. She doesn't know if her son is stuck in the storm or in a hotel room in Dillon with—" He stopped before he said more.

Hearing those word brought a flame of anger into Ashley and her face dampened either from the heat of the fire or the heat in her heart. Maybe both. It was bad enough the thoughtless knucklehead had broken her heart, but torturing his poor mother was beyond words. She almost hoped he and Jessica were stuck in a snowbank somewhere, with frostbite nipping at their fingers and toes enough to make them miserable. Just like his mother. It's what they deserved.

Brett finished his chore. "You should get some rest. The storm will probably blow itself out tonight and tomorrow you can go home."

"I'll sleep out here tonight and tend the fire. I turned the heat off in my suite."

"Suit yourself." The muffled sound of straining came from the hallway. Brett looked that way and smiled. "We may have a new guest before the night is over. I'll check and see if Linda needs a hand." He wished her a good night and left.

The fire danced and flickered, casting dancing shadows on the walls. The flames mesmerized her. The yellow and orange dancing around, with an occasional blue flicker of flame close to the logs. They popped and crackled as embers glowed a bright orange that snaked around the base of the fire. She couldn't take her eyes off the light show.

As the fire died down, she came out of her trance to add more firewood. Looking around, she noticed the tree sparkled with the firelight. Brightly colored presents circled the bottom of the tree. Many of them were probably the ones the designated elf had placed after the children were in bed. To make Christmas morning even better, her gifts should be added to the pile. She ran to get them.

A wall of cold air hit her as she opened the door to the honeymoon suite. Setting her lantern on the dresser, she stacked the gift boxes so she could carry them better. A quick change of name tags made Brandon's plush robe into a gift for David. The warm gloves for Jessica would fit Linda well, and Joe's Denver Broncos fluffy throw would be gifted to Brett. Joe's snarky attitude had landed him on the naughty list. A sock full of coal was appropriate for him.

The problem was Molly and Keisha. All she had left were the earrings she'd bought for Jessica to wear for the wedding, hardly appropriate for a little girl. But they were packaged inside a little red Christmas stocking that had a snowflake embroidered on it. Brandon's gift for Joe was inside a green Christmas stocking with a reindeer on it.

Ashley dumped the contents of the stockings into her luggage. Rummaging through her purse, she found two ten-dollar bills and put one inside each stocking. Money. The universal gift. Even five-year old girls would love that.

Three trips were required to get all the gifts back under the tree. Each trip required going past the door where the woman was struggling to give birth. The sounds coming out were enough to convince her never to have children.

After her last trip, she stood back and looked at the circle of gifts. The child inside her thrilled at the sight of so many gifts. She'd told the girls Santa would find them. The many gifts would prove that he did. The magic of Christmas was intact.

Chapter 7

. ∙ . ∙ . ♥ . ∙ . ∙ .

Ashley's flannel pajamas felt soft against her achy, tired body. Whether on a cot or the sofa, being horizontal was her greatest wish at the moment, with her eyes closed and her mind deaf to the noise inside it. With her blanket over her shoulder and her pillow under her arm, her slippers scuffed along the carpet toward the banquet hall.

Turning the corner into the large room, the target of her march was guarded by David, pacing in front of the fireplace. As soon as she saw her, he rushed to her. "I need your help. Joe and the college kids broke into my storeroom where I keep the alcohol."

Holding up her hands in front of her face, she knew what would come next.

"They're completely snockered."

He didn't need to say more. A growl erupted from the magma pool inside Ashley. Leave it to Joe to find a way to ruin the peace and quiet and drag co-conspirators in with him. Her craving for sleep would have to wait to be satisfied.

"They were mad that I caught them," he told her. "They want to be left in there for the night, but I can't do that. Bring your lantern."

"I suppose alcohol poisoning is not part of their thinking, either," she said, remembering an acquaintance from college who drank himself to death. Throwing her bedding on the sofa to claim it before others could, she sighed. "Let's go get them. I'll get Joe. You work on the college kids."

Sounds of drunken laughter and slurred singing could be heard as Ashley and David passed through the kitchen. A discarded pry bar lay outside a door, the door jamb splintered and broken. Dollar signs flashed in front of Ashley's eyes. Joe or Brandon would be paying for a new door.

The small room reeked of vomit and alcohol. Ashley put her hand over her mouth and nose, afraid to breath in the stench. The battery lantern sat on an empty shelf. Tristan and Cole lay motionless in the corner, beer bottles strewn about them. Ed sat near them in a puddle of vomit, barely able to sit up straight.

Joe stood in the middle of the room with his red Santa sweatshirt on, a bottle of whiskey held high over his head. "I won!" he proclaimed as he wobbled in his personal earthquake, teetering as if about to crash. "I'm the king of booze!"

Unable to stand it any longer, Ashley stepped outside the room and took a breath. As David joined her, she told him, "I'm sorry. We'll pay for everything."

He rubbed his furrowed brow. "First things first. I'll tell Brett so he can make sure none of those four is so drunk they're in danger. Get the king to go to his room so he can sleep it off." He took off without waiting for her answer.

Probably good that he did because she couldn't argue. Taking a deep breath, she went back into the rancid room. Grabbing him by the elbow, she told Joe, "Come on, king, let's get back to the palace."

"I'mmmm not done here." He pulled his arm away.

Impatience and anger gave her strength. She took his elbow again, ignored his whining about it hurting, and drug him out of the little room. Pushing him against the wall, she pinned him with her forearm across his chest. He was in no condition to resist.

"Listen, you drunken skunk. You're going to be quiet so you don't wake anyone. You're going to your room and going to bed. Understand me?"

"You the boss of me?" He wobbled and she pinned him harder so he wouldn't fall.

"Yes, I am."

His glazed eyes stared at her. "Okay, then."

Backing away slightly to make sure he could stand, she let him loose. He put his finger across his lips and gave a lengthy shhhhhh. With a roll of her eyes, they staggered and stumbled through the kitchen. Brett and David came through the door right before they got to it. She motioned them on as Joe asked her which door to go through.

"There's only one."

A loud slurred laugh and a protracted shhhhh heralded their arrival in the hallway. Banging from side to side, they followed the lanterns beam of light and made their way to Joe's room.

The key. She hadn't thought about getting a key, and she didn't want to feel through his pockets to look for one. With a quick prayer, she turned the knob and the door opened for them. Hallelujah! Something had gone right.

One long stumbling stride and Ashley let go of her cargo. Joe crashed on the bed facedown. Fearing he would suffocate, she tried to roll him over. Rolling a tree trunk would have been easier, but she managed to get him turned over and halfway on the bed. Lifting his feet, she slid him up on the mattress. He looked uncomfortable but that wasn't her worry. He was in the bed and could sleep off his inebriation. She piled two thick blankets on top of him.

"He did it for you," Joe said in a voice as thick as molasses. "And his mother."

Uncertain of whether he was speaking to her or talking in his sleep, she stopped to listen as he bounced around on the bed, getting in a more comfortable position.

"He loves you enough not to hurt you, but not enough to marry you." A drunken laugh came out from under the pile of blankets. "So he took off for my pal Tony's house last night." He threw back the covers and sat up. "And you know what they're doing there? Playing video games and drinking beer. I could have been there, but nooooo, I had to stay behind to deliver the note."

Ashley's heart stood as still as she did. Were her ears hearing correctly? Were these the words of a drunk or someone who knew what he was talking about? "Wait. What do you mean he's at your pal's house?"

Glazed eyes stared at her as a deep guttural laugh came out. "Yep. He's been texting me about who won the video game contest. While he's havin' a good time there, I'm stuck here with his whiny momma and you. I been cheated! I wanna go there. I'm gonna. Why should I stay here. I'm gonna go to Tony's house. It's only a couple miles from here." He slammed his fist on the bed. "And I'm gonna go there right now." He struggled to get up. He teetered a moment. "I'll go right after I puke." He gagged.

With speed that would rival Superman, she grabbed a trash can and held it in front of him as he spewed a putrid mix of beer and stomach acid.

After quietly adding more wood to the fire, Ashley lay on the sofa and rubbed at the aching in her temples. Breathing sounds came from behind the sofa where an unknown number of people slept on the cots. An occasional snore would sound out, disturbing the rhythmic breathing, but would settle down again.

After Joe's disgusting episode, she settled him down and left him in his bed sound asleep and snoring. His revelation of the conspiracy surrounding the wedding decimated the thin line between love and hate. Maybe it was a good thing Brandon was somewhere else. The images of revenge that flashed through her mind might have become reality.

Through her headache, she heard noises down the hallway again. A yelp of pain. She'd always heard it took a long time for babies to come. The noises would likely last all night long. The sounds wouldn't reach her room at the end of the hall, but she didn't want to heat that big room for only her. The generator was being taxed with running the heat, the water pump, and the kitchen. Sleeping on the sofa in front of the fireplace would suffice for tonight.

Nothing of this day had turned out as planned. Brandon wasn't worthy of her tears. She'd loved him at the start of the day. Tonight she felt nothing but revulsion for him. At the same time, if he hadn't run off, she'd be married to him. Maybe she owed him an infinitesimal debt for saving her from a miserable marriage.

Another muffled groan and sound of straining came from down the hall. The muscles in Ashley's abdomen tightened as if in sync with what she was hearing. She forced herself to relax. If there were tissues around, she'd stuff them in her ears to keep from hearing what she knew was happening. No baby was worth all that.

Unable to sleep, she got up and went to the Christmas tree. The firelight made the ornaments twinkle like stars on the massive tree, adding a touch of magic to Christmas Eve. The backdrop for her wedding ceremony was still beautiful in its decorated splendor lit only by firelight. With all the turmoil and hubbub that evening, it stood as a reminder that it was a special night. A night of peace on earth. Tranquility had finally come to the lodge.

The noise of a baby crying sounded faintly, almost as if from a dream about a long-ago night in a stable. Was she hearing that baby's cry from Bethlehem? She heard the noise again. No, it was much closer.

The baby was here! She hurried over to the room that once emanated pain and effort. Now the sounds were blissful, full of love and joy. Through the door, she heard Brett and Linda laughing softly as they talked about the new little boy checking into the lodge just before midnight.

Ashley walked back to the sofa and lay down facing the fireplace. A baby boy born on Christmas Eve. To be this close to someone just beginning their life was a first for her. His first breath was drawn in the lodge full of strangers. She hadn't seen him or knew anything about his family, but she felt a bond with the little guy in that room. She'd helped make the birthing bed for his mother. She'd brought towels for Linda to use. She'd contributed to his being here.

The warm fuzzies spread through her like a warm IV, making her eyes heavy. A day that started horribly was ending with the gentle reassurance that life would go on.

CHAPTER 8

⋅ᵥ⋅ᵥ⋅♥⋅ᵥ⋅ᵥ⋅

B right sunlight awoke Ashley as she lay on the sofa. Putting the crook of her arm over her eyes, she lay there listening to someone putting wood on the fire. She peeked out from under her arm just enough to see the time on her phone. Seven o'clock already? The night was too short, and she was still sleepy.

"Sorry, Ashley," she heard David say as he shook her foot. "Guests are stirring and will be hungry soon. Maybe your folks would let you nap in their room."

A gravelly, morning moan rose through her throat and out her lips. "Merry Christmas," she said with all the energy of a deflated balloon. She kept her eyes tightly shut. If she opened her eyes, that meant she had to leave her comfy place on the sofa and that would take more effort than she was willing to put out.

"It's a beautiful white Christmas too. Come see how beautiful the world is outside. Fresh. Untouched. Looks like a Christmas card. Look now before Brett starts plowing the snow."

His description of the sight piqued her curiosity enough that she had to see it for herself. With a yawn and a stretch, she blinked her eyes in the sunlit room. She sat up and squinted over the back of the sofa. Beyond the empty cots, the heavy drapes were drawn back, letting the solar heat and magnificent view inside. The snow glistened like piles of glitter. The trees were draped in white pillows and surrounded by unbroken drifts of snow. The mountains in the distance were white against the vibrant blue sky. Christmas Day beauty stretched out the window and into a place of special memories. Her breath left in wonderment.

A child's scream of joy drew her eyes away from the window. Several children, including Molly and Keisha, danced around the Christmas tree, excited that Santa had indeed found where they were sleeping. Smiles and family hugs from the adults added to the festive atmosphere. The sounds of joyful greetings filled the air as the rest of the guests arrived. Not wanting to be left out, Ashley joined the others in the merriment.

Maggie rushed over to Ashley and gave her a hug, then smoothed her hair down. Her father wished her a good morning. Mason stayed focused on his cell phone until Emily appeared and gave him a smile that invited him over. Accepting the invitation, he sauntered over to her to compare cell phone apps.

From the entrance to the ballroom, a Santa-hatted David gave a hearty ho-ho-ho and patted his thin belly. "Anybody here want to see what Santa brought them?"

The room filled with shouts of glee as the children danced around Santa and their parents looked on with beaming smiles. The Christmas spirit filled the room and everyone's hearts. Ashley joined the crowd, enjoying their raucous surprise and laughter as they opened gifts.

"Nice to see everyone having a good time." Brett leaned into Ashley, giving her a friendly shoulder bump. He had his outside overalls on and heavy snow boots. "I hope they leave with a good impression of us. Maybe they'll even come back when things are up and running again."

"I hope they come back too. This place is too special not to come again." She looked at his attire. "Going somewhere?"

"Jim the patrolman," he said as put on his gloves, "said the plows are out in full force on the interstate and will have it open by noon. I'm getting our tractor to plow out the parking lot and the road to the interstate. But first I'll have to shovel our entrance and sidewalk, then do the same to the doors of the shed to get the tractor out. I'd better get busy before we get a search-and-rescue call." He put his heavy stocking hat on. "If they do, I guess you'll have to finish for me." He laughed and gave her a wink.

He turned to go, but Ashley caught him by the arm. "I happen to know Santa left you a present. You should open it before you go."

With a quizzical look in his eye, he pointed a finger at his chest. "Me? I thought for sure I was on Santa's naughty list."

"Who says you aren't," David said as he walked up with Ashley's relabeled present and a twinkle in his eye. "Evidently someone snuck one by Santa."

With a pretentious laugh, he took the large box and unwrapped it with the gusto of a child. He pulled out the blue and orange Denver Bronco blanket out of its plastic case with the flourish worthy of a matador and let out a pleased cry. "Look at this! This is great! I can wear it around my Cowboys-fan wife and she'll be totally jealous."

Ashley put her hand over her mouth. "Oops, I may have accidently spread family discord."

Brett threw the blanket over his shoulder and gave her hug. "Only good-hearted discord. Not sure how you knew I was a Bronco fan, but thanks a lot. I'll have it for watching the games next season."

"I thought everyone around here would be a Broncos fan. Who isn't?"

"Linda," the men spoke in unison.

David slapped Brett on the back. "They didn't make the playoffs this year. Guess you'll have to cheer for Dallas instead." Laughing, he went back to the others.

"Never," Brett said lowly. "I gotta get to work. Thanks, Ashley, it was very nice of you. Could you give this to Linda and make sure she doesn't throw it in the trash?" He winked at her again before he disappeared out the front door. The sound of a shovel scraping against concrete came through the door as he went to work.

Folding the throw back into a neat square proved more difficult than she thought. With a last push and a tug on the zipper, she got it back into its case with the hope that the fluffy fabric wouldn't wrinkle. Taking it into the kitchen, she found Linda admiring her new leather gloves.

"I love them!" Linda said as she hugged Ashley. "I don't have any quite this nice for driving. It's so thoughtful of you!" In spite of dark circles under her eyes, her face was radiant.

"Glad you like them. Here's what I got for Brett. I'm not sure you'll be so happy with me when you see it."

Linda looked at the package as she took it by three fingers like it was made of manure. "I recognize those colors and I don't like them." She gave Ashley a little shrug and a little smile.

Running a hand through her hair, she told her, "I promised Brett you wouldn't throw it away. Please don't make a liar out of me."

Linda laughed and threw it on the counter. "I won't, but I'll give him grief for it. Good-fun grief. Everyone knows I'm a die-hard Cowboy fan, and we have a lot of fun with it during football season."

Relief swept through her. She could keep her promise. Linda would keep the throw, if for no other reason than for taunting her husband about his team's missing the playoffs. Brett would have to deal with it.

"So you delivered a baby last night."

Wiping her hands on her apron, Linda's face broke into a smile. "Cutest little boy I've ever seen. Fat and healthy and strong. His mama is doing fine. I checked on her this morning and she was feeding the baby. They both took right to it."

Not really knowing what that meant for sure, Ashley decided not to ask for the details. "Need some help with breakfast?" The counters were covered in breakfast pastries and fruit ready to be served.

"Sure! These platters of pastries and rolls need to go out to the banquet hall. I already took out the coffee urn, cups, plates, and napkins. I'm glad your wedding party was to be served a continental breakfast. Makes this morning's breakfast very easy."

The platters were light and easy to carry. Ashley took two and backed through the kitchen doors. She almost tripped over Molly who was waving a ten-dollar bill and bouncing around her.

"Look what Santa brought me! I'm rich!" She danced around Ashley, singing and waving. And hitting the edge of the platter.

Ashley felt the platter start to slip. A gasp, a rush of adrenaline, and slight of hand helped her regain control. "Molly, please go play by the tree while I serve breakfast."

Without an apology or recognition of the near disaster, Molly skipped away, calling for Keisha to come play with her. Mirroring Molly, Keisha danced around with her own ten-dollar bill.

As soon as the platters were on the table, they drew a crowd. She hurried back to the kitchen and followed Linda out, each with two more platters and a tub of fruit. The sunshine seemed to have lightened the mood of everyone who visited like they were old acquaintances. They all teased Jim about not eating too many donuts before he started his shift again. He took the ribbing well, adding his own versions of police jokes.

Ashley's cup of liquid caffeine and plate full of sugar rush kickstarted her blood flow and made her think more clearly. Today meant going home to her apartment where half of the things were Brandon's. Living there while they looked for their first home seemed like a good idea at the time. As soon as possible, he'd have to get his stuff out, or he might find it scattered across the lawn out front. After that, he should get out of her life. None of that sounded very easy. Or pleasant. Maybe he'd move out while she wasn't there. She didn't care where he went as long as it was away.

Pushing the distasteful thoughts away, she focused on the crowd around her. Torn wrapping paper littered the floor around the tree. Lanterns no longer needed were lined up on a table. Randy sat at a table with the two truckers while Maggie visited with Will and Myra. Molly and Keisha sat at the edge of the fireplace comparing ten-dollar bills. Mason and Emily sat in a corner. Amazingly, Mason didn't have earbuds in, but instead, seemed rapt on the girl's every word. Out of the corner of her eye, she saw Linda take a small plate of pastries down the hall. A mother who took to feeding her baby likely would take to some breakfast as well.

Missing but unmissed were Joe, Tristan, Cole, and Ed. No doubt still sleeping off their midnight binges. No telling when they'd finally get up. Maybe David would check on them later to make sure everyone was okay.

Rhonda sat in the corner, her bleary, red-rimmed eyes and hand-wringing tugged at Ashley's heart. Bob brought her a croissant, but she waved it off. Taking a step toward her, Ashley was ready to repeat what she'd learned from Joe. Not knowing how Rhonda or Bob would react stopped her short. Tattletales usually had things come back on them, so maybe it was best to let Brandon explain himself. She couldn't because she didn't understand it.

A shoulder hug and a smile bought a surprised look to the Colemans' faces as she sat down. Leaning in, she told them, "Don't worry. Brandon is fine. They'll find him today and he'll be with you soon. I'm sure of it."

Rhonda's eyebrows shot up as high as they would go. "And you know this how? Is there something you know that we don't?"

Her heart pounded so loudly in her ears, Ashley could barely hear herself think about how to get out of this unpleasant situation. Her mouth was dry and her face felt hot. "I—I meant the plows are out. I'm thinking—I'm sure they'll find anyone stranded. Or maybe he's waiting for you at your house." She stood. "Excuse me. I see someone I want to talk to." Quickly rising, she rushed away.

The lie seemed better than the truth. She'd said too much when she really wanted to wash her hands of the whole affair.

David was nowhere to be seen. She needed to talk to him. His gentle presence and level head made her feel safe amid all this madness. In all the hubbub of the storm and cancelled wedding, they'd talked a little. His warmth toward her and kind words had made the situation bearable. His cool head and consideration of his guests was the antithesis of Brandon. Brandon would never be like his father, no matter how long she waited for it. But David already had the qualities she admired most. A warm flow spread through her chest, down her arms, and up into her brain.

The sensation made her stop. She was on the rebound, as she often heard it put. Any strange emotional stirrings were probably due to her unconscious searching for something to fill the void Brandon left. She'd promised herself not to fall in love again and she meant it. David was being nice to her because he felt sorry for her. She was a guest that needed special attention and he provided it. It was part of the price in renting the lodge. Customer service at its best. Her eyes stung, and she squeezed them tight to keep the tears safely inside.

Just a few more hours and she'd get to go home. The lodge was no longer a place of refuge, but a place of bad memories and where her heart played games with her. Being home would help her get back on track. She didn't need anyone to provide happiness. It was all up to her now. She'd meet the challenge head-on and succeed.

CHAPTER 9

L inda laughed out loud as she picked up the large kettle off the gas stove. She poured the kettle's contents into an urn of coffee for the guests.

David looked up from the platters he'd brought in from the banquet hall. "What's so funny?"

"You! You're humming Christmas tunes. You haven't done that in years." She leaned toward him, looking out of the side of her eyes. "And you have a certain look about you. Why are you so happy? Could it be a rejected bride is available for courting and you're hoping to do it?"

David kept his eyes focused on the dishes he was washing as he cleared his throat. "I don't know what you mean." He put the dishes into a hot tub of water and swirled the hot water around them. He'd blame the heat in his cheeks on the steam. The last thing he wanted exposed were his feelings for Ashley.

He felt a bump at his side. Linda pushed him aside to finish the dishwashing chore. "I know you like her. She's a sweet lady, and Molly certainly likes her. You'd be crazy not to get friendly with her."

Too late. The lodge wasn't a good place to keep secrets. People were too close.

"It's too soon for her. Once the dust settles, maybe I'll run into her again. If I offer her a free night's stay, maybe she'll come back." He picked up a towel and dried the plates after Linda rinsed them.

"Making a plan. That's good."

The door from the back room banged open and Brett came running in. He grabbed David's arm, nearly knocking the plate out of his hands.

"Come with me," he said in a low tone. "I need your help outside." His firm stare had a tinge of fear in it. "Hurry! Linda, bring the EMS kit!"

David tossed the towel to Linda who dried her hands. Brett was already on his way out the door as they put their snow gear on before running out into the tracks Brett had made. He'd shoveled a path from the front door of the lodge to the sidewalk. One pass through the parking lot with the tractor had cleared a wide path. The tractor sat near the other end, close to where Brett was kneeling.

As they came running up, Brett said, "I didn't see him until I turned back. I saw something red sticking out from behind his car. That's when I stopped to investigate, and this is what I found." He stepped aside, revealing the partially buried body of Joe. A sweatshirt and underwear were the only things he wore.

"Oh, dear Lord," David muttered as he dropped to his knees and started pushing away the snow.

Brett grabbed under Joe's armpits and pulled him out from between the cars.

Linda pulled out a stethoscope and handed it to Brett, then pulled out a space blanket. "David, go get that sled so we can get him to the lodge."

Thankful to be given a meaningful action, he headed for the back of the inn. No one had died at the lodge before. Not even the elderly guests he'd hosted. To have someone die because he didn't secure his liquors well enough was incomprehensible. Whatever needed to be done to prevent it from happening again would be done.

He grabbed the rope tied to the sled and ran back to the others as fast as his snowsuit would allow him to go. "Is he still alive?"

"Barely. I'm not sure he'll even make it back to the lodge, but we must get him warmed up. We can handle this. Go get Jim. He'll need to file a report in case he dies."

Running again while saying a fervent prayer, David rushed in the doorway. Unwilling to cause alarm, he shed the top of his snowsuit and looked in the door of the banquet hall for Jim. Catching Jim's eye, he signaled for him to come. A few others observed the action and started to rise from their chairs. Motioning downward with his hands, they sat back down.

Jim had on his official demeanor as he stepped into the entrance. "Problem?"

Quickly explaining what had happened, David opened the door just as Brett pulled the sled under the porte-cochère. Linda left the others and ran into the lodge.

"Is he still alive?" Jim asked as he knelt across the sled from Brett.

"Not sure. Let's take him in front of the fireplace. It's the warmest place in the lodge. Say a prayer. This guy is as close to dying as I've ever seen."

Brett took the upper part of Joe while Jim got between his legs and lifted them. David held the door as they went inside and into the banquet hall.

Chaos and screaming were immediate. Chairs were knocked over as people stood. Families sought each other and clung together.

Running to a cot that still had bedding flung on it, David got the blanket and spread it in front of the fireplace. Shouting instructions to his guests to leave the banquet hall unless they were willing to help, he herded out those who didn't leave out into the hallway.

"Randy. Bob. We need some sheets off beds and more blankets. Bring them in so we can try to get him warm. Hurry!" The men, followed by Will, ran to gather the items.

David returned to the banquet hall and put more wood on the fire. Linda brought in a pot of water and set it near the coals. Brett had cut away the sweatshirt. Joe's hands and feet were blue, providing the only color on the white body. Putting the stethoscope on Joe's chest, Brett listened. The rest of them stood breathless, praying he would hear something.

Sitting up, Brett announced, "His heart is barely beating. It's likely his organs have begun or have already shut down." He looked up at Linda. "Did you call for LifeFlight?"

She nodded.

Randy, Will, and Bob came running in with sheets and blankets. Soon a tent of sheets concentrated heat from the fireplace to the floor in front of it. Other guests came to help hold it in place. The water in the pot by the coals was hot so Linda dipped small towels in it and put the warmed towels under Joe's arms. At Brett's instruction, Bob took off his shirt and lay beside the frozen body under a blanket. When he could no longer stand it, Randy took his place.

One of the truckers holding a corner of the sheet asked, "What was Joe doing outside in nothing but a sweatshirt and his underwear?"

Everything in David froze, including his brain. If he'd put on a better door, this would have never happened. He'd never planned on such a determined alcoholic going after his stores like Joe had done. This was his own fault. A sober Joe would have never tried to go outside dressed like that.

Looking up from where he knelt on the floor, Brett replied, "He vandalized the storeroom where we keep the liquor and proceeded to drink himself into oblivion. He was wasted so there's no telling what he was thinking. I doubt he knows." He put the stethoscope to his ears and went back to work.

Decked out in his police uniform, Jim chimed in. "I've seen it a lot. That's what too much liquor will do to you. Kill you. I'm glad he wasn't driving, or he might have killed others."

Much to David's relief, no more questions came about what Joe was doing. No one could argue with Brett or Jim. Joe brought this on himself and everyone knew it.

His arm was going numb holding the sheet up against the fireplace. He shifted his weight to take some of the pressure off his one leg. As he moved a little, he caught sight of Ashley standing pale against the wall by the Christmas tree. Her lips moved in silent prayer. Her eyes stared unblinking at the scene. He knew she blamed herself for Joe.

When Stanley Mortimer asked if he could help, David gladly relinquished his post. Handing Stanley the edge of the sheet, he added another piece of firewood before going to Ashley. He couldn't help himself as he put her arm around her. The floodgate of tears opened as she leaned against him, causing him to hold her closer. While she released her guilt, he savored holding her close.

As her sobbing slowed, she choked out, "He said he wanted to go to Tony's house. I never thought he'd try. I left him sleeping. I thought he'd sleep until morning."

"His outdoor venture wasn't your fault. He was too drunk to know what he was doing."

"But if he dies—"

"It will be by his own hand. We did all we could do for him."

Sniffing, she pulled away from him. "I guess you're right."

"Of course, I am." Giving her his handkerchief, he nodded toward the fireplace. "Has Jim talked to you yet?"

"Yes. I told him everything."

Nodding, he gave her a shoulder hug. "I should get back there."

As he walked away, a tug on his shirt made him stop. A "thank you" meant only for his ears made him smile and gave him courage to face the struggle to save a life.

While Jim completed his part of the investigation, several of the male guests took turns lying next to Joe, trying to warm him up. Hot water bottles were places in his armpits and hot air was fanned on him. He never regained consciousness, but his white skin turned not-as-white. Brett thought his heart was beating a little better, but there was no way to know what damage his internal organs had suffered, if any.

The LifeFlight air ambulance dispatched from Denver landed about an hour after they found him. The guests of the lodge watched from the windows as it lifted off and headed to the hospital. Brett headed down the hallway to make sure Tristan, Cole, and Ed had survived the night.

The buzz of conversation and sharing of interpretations of what happened grew in volume. No longer strangers, his guests talked and clung to each other and bonded over their shared experience. None of them would forget their stay at Spruce Canyon Lodge. His only hope was that they wouldn't think badly of him and the lodge.

Although he was happy to provide shelter, he wondered if any of them would come back. Return customers were the biggest part of his business. Some of them he'd rather not see again, like the three college boys. When Brett returned with a thumbs up and a smirk, he knew they were alive but suffering severe hangovers.

While relieved that they were fine, he was glad they were suffering. Served them right.

And where was Molly? He hadn't seen her since breakfast. Molly had been left on her own too much the past two days. No telling what mischief she'd invented, especially if egged on by Keisha. Cleaning up her messes seemed like nothing compared to what he was facing now. Cots, sheets, blankets, pillows, and food service items littered the floor and most of the horizontal surfaces in the banquet hall. Utter disarray. His cleaning people would faint when they saw the state of the lodge.

His fixation on the lodge was interrupted.

"Hi, Daddy. Where you been?"

Innocent eyes looked up at him and deep into his soul. Too many responsibilities had caused him to neglect her this Christmas day. Their days together would end soon enough. Since Monica died, he'd been aware of how short and precious time with family was, and he'd promised never to take it for granted. He wouldn't let that happen again.

"Why're you looking at me like that, Daddy?"

Kneeling down, he told her, "Did I wish you a merry Christmas?" He gathered her in his arms and squeezed until she protested. "Tell me what Santa brought you for Christmas."

"I will but first, tell me why you hugged Ashley for so long. Do you like her?"

Staring at his daughter didn't make her question go away. His daughter missed nothing. This old soul in a small package wanted an honest answer. She'd know if he were lying. "Yes, I do."

CHAPTER 10

⋅▾⋅▾⋅♥⋅▾⋅▾⋅

Ashley was vaguely aware of her parents packing suitcases and gathering her things from the bridal suite. The view from her parent's room was beautiful. Curving snowbanks and snow-laden evergreens extended far into the distance, ending below the snow-capped peak and blue skies. The afternoon sunlight made the wisps of windblown snowflakes sparkle like glitter caught in the breeze. She saw none of it.

Images of Brandon swirled in her mind. Their childhood days, their high school experiences, their courtship through college, their plans to blend their lives even tighter. Where she once felt fiery cold, she now felt uncertain about everything. In the last two days, she'd felt loved, hurt, betrayed, and angry. She'd wanted Brandon to suffer for what he'd done to her, but seeing Joe lying there made her rethink her need for retribution. She'd never liked Joe because he'd moved Brandon away from her, but she'd never wished him dead.

"Come on, honey," her father crooned, "it's time to go home." He put his hand under her arm to help lift her from the chair.

Like a dead phone suddenly plugged into power, she awoke out of her daydream. "I don't want to leave yet." The words surprised her. She hadn't thought them before they spilled out, but she agreed with them. Some small flicker of light inside made her feel that it wasn't time for her to leave. There was something here she still needed to do. Confused, but determined, she insisted, "I'm staying another night."

"We've already cleaned out your room and packed everything."

"Put it back."

Maggie towered in front of her daughter. "Don't be silly, Ashley. You've had a terrible shock and need to rest. You need to go home with us. We can wait for news of Brandon and Jessica together at home. I'll help you get the wedding gifts ready to send back."

"If she wants to stay, Maggie, let her. If they find him near here, she'd be close by to see him."

"She doesn't want to see him."

"How do you know? Did she tell you that?"

Their noise went on, like a grinding wheel against metal. Now she knew why she needed to stay here. To escape the nagging and bickering of her parents once they got home. She needed peace and quiet to sort things out for herself. That flicker in her chest grew. The last place she needed to be was with her parents.

"I'm staying one more night," she said above the noise of her parents. Gritting her teeth for a few seconds kept harsher words inside her. She took a deep breath. "I have my car. I'll go home tomorrow. Please go. Leave me in peace. I have a lot of thinking to do."

"See what you've done, Randy! You made her mad."

"I did not! You did! She got upset when you talked about returning the wedding gifts. What are you thinking?"

"Someone has to bring it up."

The arguing continued, but Ashley's attention to them stopped. Something inside her told her to stay. Something unexplainable but absolute. Maybe it was the call of the hot tub that was now operational with the power being restored. Maybe it was the quiet of the bridal suite where her mind was free to think without interruption. Maybe she didn't want to face her apartment that had hers and Brandon's things in it. No matter. One more day was needed before facing her fluid and unplanned future.

A movement beside her interrupted her musings. Mason leaned on the window sill facing Ashley. He had a crooked smile on his face. "For fifty bucks, I'll get them out of your hair."

Amusement at his remark forced a faint smile. "Your price has gone up."

He crossed his arms and smirked. "They're gonna argue with you until you go, unless I work on them."

"But fifty dollars! Last time, it cost me twenty. How about thirty?"

An eyeroll signaled his rejection of the offer.

"Forty?"

"Fifty and I'll have them out of here within an hour."

"Done."

With a shrug and a smirk, he stood up. "Mom. Dad. Instead of arguing about Ashley, you should go see if you can drive the

Colemans home. I'm sure they're in no shape to drive back to Denver."

An immediate halt of the debate took effect. Maggie put her fingers over her mouth and paced a couple of laps. "You're right, Mason. Ashley, you're on your own. You seem to be handling things better than they are. Come on, Bob, let's go see if we can help them back home." She gathered up a few things and went out the door.

Bob crossed his arms and gave his son a sideways glance before picking up a suitcase. "How much did she pay you this time?"

"Fifty."

Tipping the large bag, Bob said, "I'll throw in another ten for getting your mom off on another mission so fast. Ashley, honey, will you be okay if we leave?"

"Yeah, Dad. I need some time to myself." She crossed the room to him and planted a kiss on his cheek. "Take the wedding gown with you please."

He nodded as he took the handle of a large suitcase and threw the large, very-stuffed garment bag over his shoulder. "Mason, get the rest of the bags and let's take them to the car."

Ashley held the door for them as they left the room with their load of luggage. While she loved her family, time without them around would help her think things through and organize a to-do list. Staying an extra night meant she was free to be a guest and enjoy the comforts of her room. But first, she probably needed permission to stay. David was her first stop.

Following her family down the hallway, she saw Uncle Don visiting with Brett by the reception desk. She called out to him before he joined the family to head back to Denver. A smile crossed his face as he dropped his luggage and came her way.

"I was hoping I'd see you before we left. How you doing, Sweetpea?"

His use of her childhood nickname warmed her insides like a cup of hot chocolate. "Doing fine, Uncle Don. I need time to think about where to go from here. I'll come back tomorrow."

He leaned in close to her. "How much did you have to pay for your alone-time?"

They both laughed. "Fifty, but well worth it. If I haven't said it before, thanks for getting whatever paperwork you needed to marry us. I'm sorry it didn't work out."

"I'll save it for next time."

Not wanting to disappoint him with her decision to stay single, she nodded and gave him a hug and a peck on the cheek. With luggage in hand, he turned to give her a smile before following the family out the door.

Alone at last, she went back down the hallway, passing the Mortimers as they left their room. The college boys came out of their room looking like zombies from a B movie. Stanley was driving them back to their dorm. From the bedraggled look of them, they were in no shape to drive. Or ride for that matter. If Stanley was smart, he'd take buckets or bags for any stomach contents that might arise.

Out of one of the rooms, Molly came skipping merrily along trailing the veil behind her as she sang a made-up song about being a superhero princess. With the edges of the veil held out, she spun, then stuck her arms in front of her and made a swishing noise as she raced down the corridor. She came to a sudden stop in front of Ashley. Taking the Wonder-Woman stance, she said, "I'm here to rescue you!"

A smile spread across Ashley's face. This child was truly a rescuer. She could find David and request another night of lodging for her. Her father wouldn't resist the request if it came from this veil-clad superhero. She hoped.

"Super-Duper Girl, could you find the man who owns this lodge and ask him if I can stay in the honeymoon suite for one more night? I'll pay for the extra night if he says yes. You'd be my true hero if you did that for me."

A wild jump in the air followed by a hoot of joy echoed down the hall. "Yes!" Myra Dugan poked her head out of her room to see what was going on. She smiled as she watched the girl flash by.

Gathering her luggage outside of her family's room door, Ashley toted it back to the honeymoon suite. Unpacking seemed premature since she didn't know for sure if David would agree to her staying. Her leggings and a heavy sweater would be more comfortable than the jeans and sweatshirt she wore. Quickly changing, she decided to go find David herself. It was better than waiting for Super-Duper Girl to fly back with news.

She was halfway down the hall when she saw Molly running toward her. The look on her face was not one of glee but of concern.

"Daddy says come quick. Some people are here asking for you."

"Some people?"

"Yeah, a man and a lady. They were here before."

Brandon and Jessica. Had to be. No, no, no. She wasn't ready to see them yet. She hadn't had time to think out what she'd say to them. She needed more time. But they were here, seeking her out. What was it Uncle Don told her? She'd have the advantage if she faced them on her ground. With no excuse to avoid them any longer, she willed her frozen limbs to carry her forward.

Molly led her to the entrance to the banquet hall and stopped. Pointing inside, she said, "Daddy says I can't go in there, and I can't listen either. But you have to go in."

Rounding the corner, she saw Jessica sitting on the sofa and Brandon standing beside the fireplace. They looked up at her as she entered the room, but immediately looked down. Jessica rubbed her tension-creased forehead. Brandon's jaw muscles worked overtime.

The standoff was deafeningly silent. Not wanting to look at her former friends, Ashley looked at her feet, warm and snug in her fleece-lined boots. All the things to say jumbled together so that nothing fit together well enough to speak. Forgiveness and anger struggled for control over which would be set free.

Brandon broke the silence. "I'm sorry."

Tears immediately fell from Ashley's eyes onto her boots. This wasn't how she wanted this to go. Tears ceded her power over the situation. Having seen napkins left over from breakfast still on the table, she turned and went there to get one. Wiping her eyes helped her regain control so that she could confront them from a position of power.

Turning, she faced them, chin up and shoulders back. Crossing her arms, she stared at them. "You heard about Joe?"

Nodding, Brandon said David had informed them of his status. "But enough of him." Brandon took a step toward her. "I'm sorry. I was wrong to do what I did. Can you forgive me?"

It was a loaded question. Saying no would imply she was so angry she'd never get over it. Saying yes might make him think there was hope for reconciliation. There wasn't. No matter his eyes pleading for her to come back to him. No matter his slightly shaking hands or slightly damp upper lip showing how badly he wanted it.

The only thing she really wanted to know, she asked him. "Tell me why you left."

When he made a move to step closer to her, she narrowed her eyes and he stopped. Space between them was better than having him close. She might weaken.

Brandon looked at his hands and rubbed them together. He didn't make eye contact as he told her his side of the issue. "I got cold feet. Joe convinced me I hadn't dated around enough to know who I wanted to spend my life with." Finally looking at her, he added, "He can be a very persuasive guy."

Unimpressed, Ashley kept her poker face on and her arms crossed.

Looking away, he rubbed he back of his neck. "I have no excuse. I panicked and ran. I'm sorry." He closed the space between them and whispered, "I still love you. I still want to marry you. I promise, I'll never run away again for as long as I live." Holding his hand out in invitation for hers, he paused.

The familiar hand beckoned her. It would be easy. But it would be wrong. The love she had for him had not been extinguished but weakened to the point of no recovery. Her heart told her it was over.

Moving only her eyes, she looked at Jessica on the sofa. "And you. Why?"

"I did it for you."

Jessica rose and slowly walked toward Ashley as she talked. "I heard them talking about you. Joe kept telling Brandon not to rush into marriage. That there were too many fish out there..." she waved her arm in a wide circle, "...that should be checked out before settling down to a frump like you."

Brandon swung around. "Those were his words. Not mine!"

Instead of talking to Ashley, Jessica spoke to Brandon. "But you didn't argue with him. If that's what he thought, why was he even here?"

Brandon didn't answer her question but looked away.

Coming closer, Jessica faced off with him. "I also heard them talking about the girls they brought up here before. Did you tell Ashley about them?"

The color of his face turned white, followed by the red with the blush of embarrassment at being caught. His arms hung limp at his side as his head hit his chest in humiliation. He looked from one woman to the other and back again, slouching, then standing up straight. If he was searching for some iota of support, none was found. His eyes moistened as he came near to Ashley. He held out his hands again, repeating his request to hold hers.

Giving him her hands would bring back too many memories that she wasn't prepared to face. She tucked her hands behind her crossed arms.

Giving up, he confessed, "I've been wrong about a lot of things. Joe got me so confused, telling me I should leave you. I shouldn't have listened to him. I should have walked away from him, not you. I'm sorry for being so dumb."

Jessica wasn't through. "You are dumb! So back to my story." She turned toward Ashley. "I overheard too much so they made me go with Brandon to someone's house who lives near here."

Ashley's jaw dropped. "They kidnapped you?"

Shaking her head, Jessica continued, "I knew if I went along with them, the wedding would be off, and after what I heard, I couldn't let you go through with it."

Relief spread through Ashley like a gentle rain. Her maid of honor had regained her honor, and their friendship was still intact.

Brandon raked his hand through his mussed hair as Jessica went on. "To his credit, Brandon had no idea what we were walking into. It was like a frat house. Booze and video games. They were mad because their girlfriends couldn't get there because of the storm.

They started whispering about getting me drunk and well, you can imagine the rest. I locked myself in the bedroom and barricaded the door. I heard Brandon through the door challenging them to video games, poker, and anything else to get them away from that door."

She turned to face Brandon. "I was terrified, but knowing that you were there keeping them occupied, I wasn't as afraid as I might have been. Thank you for protecting me." Rushing at him, she embraced him in a full hug.

At first, he hesitated, but then folded his arms around her to hold her close. "There was no way I was going to let them hurt you. It was the worst night of my life. Yours too, I bet."

Nodding, she pulled away from him. "All too true." Wiping her face, she turned to the silent Ashley. "Do you forgive me?"

Nothing more than opening her arms were needed to say yes. The women hugged each other. A couple of tears and several sniffles revitalized their friendship. Pulling away, Jessica excused herself from the room, leaving the former bride and groom to talk privately.

"Ashley." Brandon sat on the edge of the sofa, positioned so he could look at her face. "I love you and I want to marry you. I've never been more certain of anything in my life. I promise I'll be faithful and do anything you want me to do. All you have to do is ask me, tell me, or demand it of me. I'll do it."

Embers burned in the fireplace, needing more wood to warm the room. Ashley threw in three logs before sitting on the sofa to watch the magic of combustion. The sides of the logs turned black as the flames licked at them. Heat, fuel, and oxygen. The three components of combustion. If any of the three were missing, the fire wouldn't burn. She'd learned that in grade school, back when she first knew Brandon. The concept was so simple yet so profound. Watching fire consume the wood seemed cathartic since her wedding had gone down in flames.

Brandon leaned down, breaking her line of sight to the fire. "Honey, did you hear me? I love you. Surely your love for me hasn't died. We loved each other enough that we decided to spend our lives together. How can that have disappeared overnight?"

Staring into his eyes, she saw the confusion he felt. He truly expected things to go back to the way they were. Just as logs couldn't unburn, their feelings before the wedding could never come back. "My feelings for you have changed because I learned new things about you, and I didn't like what I heard. They changed because you weren't honest with me. They changed because I found out I couldn't trust you. Don't you see, Brandon. Marriage is based on three things: love, trust, and honesty. Take away one of those, and the marriage won't work. You took away two of them. I deserve all three. I love you and probably always will, but not enough to marry you."

His eyes crunched down into slits as they filled with tears. His face contorted as he began to cry. "What have I done?" He covered his face with his hands and sobbed. "I messed up everything."

Ashley let him cry on her shoulder, as any friend would let another friend do. None of her tears mixed with his. Her heart felt light, free of its bonds of sorrow, cold, and anger. She was free of Brandon's hold on her. She whispered in his ear, "I forgive you."

The clock read three o'clock when she and Brandon left the banquet hall. The lodge was quiet without guests. Jessica was gone, David and Molly were nowhere to be seen, and Brett and Linda were probably in their house catching up on sleep.

Even with no witnesses, the moment was awkward. Brandon bit a fingernail as he did a dance of nervousness. Ashley had pity on him and gave him a quick hug.

"You said you'd do anything I asked you to. Did you mean it?"

Rather than voicing an answer, he nodded.

"I ask you to be a friend to Joe. He was on the brink of death and may face serious problems ahead. He needs a friend to help him through it. Maybe you can be the good influence on him that he never had."

Brandon nodded. "I can do that. I'll go see him at the hospital tomorrow."

"Good. The second thing, I'm telling you to go to my apartment get the wedding gifts from your family and friends, and return them to the senders. Your mother can help you with that."

He agreed.

"The last thing I demand of you."

One of his eyebrows raised. "Demand?"

"Your words, not mine. And remember you said you meant it."

Caught by his own words, he reluctantly agreed.

"I demand that you get all your stuff out of my apartment before I get back tomorrow afternoon. I don't care how you do it. Just do it. And don't bother anything that's mine or I will come after you."

"But—but—" Brandon's eyes widened, and his arms flailed in the air. "I can't do that. It's too big of a job to do by then. Besides, where would I go? I let my apartment go already."

Enough of her time, tears, and worry had been spent on this man. Let him figure it out. She turned and walked down the hallway, shouting over her shoulder, "Not my problem."

CHAPTER 11

The warm water of the hot tub caressed Ashley's body. Her eyes were closed as she lay back in the water, letting time slip by her like a silk scarf on her skin. No one wanted her to make a decision or do anything for them. She was alone in this quiet and serene space. Her mind emptied of worries and strain.

A soft ding gave her a few seconds warning before the jets turned off. Her time was done for this session. The water settled around her, soothing her as her body felt buoyant and free. Nothing hurried her along or weighed her down. After inspecting her fingers and toes to make sure they were adequately wrinkled, she got out.

The sky turned pink as the sun set, coloring the snow-covered landscape the same hue. The gas fireplace silently flamed as it emitted a welcome heat in the room. Pulling on a robe, she sat in a chair in front of the fire. The peace and quiet comforted her like a soft quilt. Too many people and too much drama had filled the last two days. The pandemonium would resume once she drove back to Denver, but for now, she drew strength in the serenity around her.

Closing her eyes, she snuggled down into the chair. Strange sounds came from outside her door right before an envelope slid underneath it. The last note she'd received had changed her life. Getting another one after such a tumultuous day made her leery of new notes. The only thing that could move her from her comfortable perch was curiosity, and it got the best of her.

Scooping up the envelope, she took it back to her comfortable chair. Her name was written in childlike scrawl on the envelope. Now what was Molly up to?

Opening it up, a short note was enclosed.

Ashley, Supper will be served in the banquet hall at 6:30 pm. Casual attire required. Love, Molly

Her stomach growled its response to the invitation. Breakfast was hours ago and in the flurry of finding Joe frozen in the snow, lunch had gone by without a thought. A little of her delicious wedding cake was left over. Forget about putting it under her pillow to dream of her true love, she'd rather have that piece in her stomach.

Putting on her Christmas sweater and leggings again, she left her room a little before the appointed time. No creatures stirred, and silence haunted her along the way. The long hall almost seemed spooky, like Halloween rather than festive like Christmas. She hurried to the homey banquet hall. The Christmas tree was lit up and sparkling with all its lights. The mantle over the fireplace still had stockings hanging from it. A nice fire burned in the fireplace, casting dancing shadows on the wall. The Christmas spirit still filled the empty room, bringing with it a relaxed and happy atmosphere.

Rattling and clanging broke the silence as David and Molly came in with a cart full of food and utensils. "We're having a wienie roast!" Molly yelled out as she danced around the sofa.

"Hope you don't mind a simple supper," David said as he threw a comforter on the floor. "It's our Christmas Eve tradition, but since we didn't get to do it last night, we thought it would be fun tonight. We like to think of it as an indoor picnic in the middle of winter."

"Sounds like lots of fun!"

Molly danced around them singing her own song about picnics and Santa Claus as David opened the package of wienies. She stopped the moment he pulled out the roasting sticks. Sticking a wienie on the end of a very long-handled fork, David handed it to her. Molly held it expertly over the coals on the side of the fire.

"You want one?" he asked as he put another one on another fork.

"Sure." Ashley took it from him and went to stand near the fireplace.

Molly pulled hers out of the fire and took a whiff of the wienie before putting it back near the coals. "I love hot dogs cooked on the fire, don't you, Ashley?"

"I think so. It's been so long since I had one cooked that way that I've forgotten how they taste. They smell very yummy."

A third long fork joined the fire and soon the sound of sizzling of meat could be heard alongside the fire's crackling. The hot meat was soon inside the buns, covered with mustard, cheese, and relish.

Potato salad and pickles rounded out the feast, followed by the last of the wedding cake for dessert.

David put the plates and leftovers away before getting the games out. Molly got to choose which she wanted to play. After two games of Yahtzee, she lay down on one of the blankets in front of the fireplace. Soon her breathing indicated that she'd fallen asleep.

Ashley stared at the dancing lights of the coals, watching them flicker around like they were alive.

David sat on the other end of the sofa, softly humming a tune. Then the humming stopped. "Want to talk about what's happened? What you're feeling? I'm a good listener."

She knew he wasn't prying but was genuinely interested. He was offering to carry part of the burden. His gentle spirit triggered a feeling of trust.

"I feel guilty." She held her hand up immediately to stop his arguing the point. "I feel guilty about Brandon. I feel guilty for being so blind I couldn't see what was going on." She stared at her hands with her manicured nails. "I broke his heart this afternoon, but I had to do it. I couldn't trust him anymore."

Thankful that he nodded without replying, she continued. "Jessica told me she figured out Brandon wasn't ready to get married. She didn't run away with him. She was getting him away from me so I didn't make a huge mistake."

"What?" David moved closer to her, his arm up on the back of the sofa. "So they didn't run off together?"

Ashley shook her head. "It was her way of stopping the wedding by showing me what kind of man he was." Playing with the hem of her sweater, she kept her hands busy so she wouldn't twist them as she spoke. "I despised Jessica for what she did, but she did it out of love for me. And Brandon. He's basically a good man, but he fell under the bad influence of Joe. It changed him, and he didn't know it."

Rubbing his stubble along his jawline, David said, "Wow, that's quite a turnaround from what we all thought."

"They left here and went up the road to a place one of Joe's friends owns. After listening to all of Rhonda's grieving and worry, it made me mad that Brandon was up the way a couple of miles, drinking, playing video games, and having fun. It's a terrible thing to do to your mother."

He nodded but said nothing before getting up to throw more wood on the fire.

She waited for him to sit again before going on. "Most of it is my fault. I got so caught up in my job and planning the wedding that I didn't recognize the signs that there was trouble ahead. Things shouldn't have gotten as far as they did. I was blind to all of it. There's no two ways about it. I'm a fool."

"No!" he said as he scooted closer, his arm still on the back of the sofa. "None of it was your fault. Other people made their choices without your input and you all suffered the consequences."

Her chin quivered and before she knew it, her eyes filled with unintentional tears. She hit her thigh with her fist. "I'm tired of crying about all this. I thought I was cried out and over it but look at me. Feeling sorry for myself and here they come again."

His hand brushed her shoulder. "Emotions happen, no matter what we do to control them. There's nothing wrong with crying. Letting go is often done through tears."

With her cheeks wet from tears, she looked into David's eyes lit by the dying firelight. Even in the darkness, the love in his eyes shone brightly.

He wiped her face and left his hand on the side of her head. He transmitted how he felt about her through his gentle touch.

Her future suddenly became clear. She'd wasted too much time on the illusion of love. All that she'd been hoping for was right in front of her. A man she could trust. A man who was honest with her. A man she could love.

Two arms enveloped her as the last of her tears emptied herself of grief, guilt, and wasted time. His arms were strong and reassuring. They brought solace and the hope of starting afresh. They brought comfort and an occasional soft kiss around her face. As her tears slowed, the arms brought a sense of well-being. Of being at home. She'd finally arrived at the place she was always meant to be.

She opened her mouth to say something, but he quickly smothered the words with his own mouth. A thousand sparklers lit inside her, electrifying her blood so that it pumped warmer than it ever had.

CHAPTER 12

⋅ᵥ⋅ᵥ⋅♥⋅ᵥ⋅ᵥ⋅

Christmas Eve dawned bright and sunny across a snow-covered landscape. Inside Spruce Canyon Lodge, the large Fir Christmas tree dominated one corner of the banquet hall. Next to it was a large evergreen arch decorated with white lights, voile, strings of beads, and a cluster of mistletoe. Five rows of chairs faced the arch, waiting for the wedding guests to arrive. White tablecloths and fine china covered the tables on the other end of the room.

Six-year-old Molly danced into the room, resplendent in her red frilly dress. Her hair had been curled and styled so that she looked like she was at least ten.

Linda came in behind her with a tray of flower vases. "Don't mess up your hair. Ashley doesn't have time to fix it again."

"I won't mess it up. I just wanted to see everything." She helped Linda put out the last few vases. "It looks pretty, doesn't it."

Crossing her arms, Linda surveyed the room. "It's perfect."

In her suite at the lodge, Ashley studied herself in the mirror. Today was her wedding day. No notes calling the wedding off had arrived. No blizzard raged outside to keep her guests away. No doubt touched her heart. This love was here to stay.

Her A-line, floor-length white Damask dress was accented by her Santa hat with a veil attached and a red-rose bouquet that had miniature tree ornaments in it. Bells might have been a nice touch, but she was afraid if her hands shook, the bells would be disruptive during the ceremony. Her makeup made her look beautiful, and her long, dark hair hung below the Santa cap, curled over her shoulders, and down her back. She felt like Mrs. Claus the bride.

"You look—" Maggie looked at her with one lifted eyebrow, "—like you're going to a Christmas party. And so do I." She waved her hand at her Christmas sweater over her jeans.

"We are. Christmas is a magical season. It's a season of love and good will. The perfect atmosphere for starting a new life together."

She turned to look at her parents. Randy was leaning against the door frame, his arms crossed. He seemed amused at the exchange, unwilling to step into the potential quagmire of differences between a mother's idea of a perfect wedding and a daughter's ideas for the same.

Linda stuck her head in the room. "It's time." Her face broke out in a wide smile. "You look fabulous! So festive and happy. David's a lucky man."

With a heart about to burst from holding too much happiness, Ashley moved to take her father's arm. At the entrance to the banquet hall, Molly's mouth was agape as she looked at Ashley. Her heart must have been full too because she ran and hugged Ashley. Hard. A kiss to her about-to-be daughter set her at ease. Mason took his mother's arm and escorted her to her seat, followed by Jessica in her matron-of-honor red dress and Molly who threw tinsel down the aisle before the bride.

All eyes turned to look at her as she stepped into the banquet hall. Her sisters and their families were there along with David's brother and his family. Jim was there and the Mortimers, the Dugans, and the two truckers who had been stranded at the lodge last year.

As she reached the end of the aisle, David came into view. His Santa hat, over a beaming smile, made him look like the happiest man on earth.

In the end, she got what she wanted. A Christmas Eve wedding. The love of a good man. A family.

ABOUT THE AUTHOR

The author spent her life doing many different things. She's been a wife and mother, a teacher, a statistician, a literacy tutor, timber sale accountant, an archeological technician, and a technical writer/editor. Now retired, she loves to quilt, sew, and write in her home in the hills where the bison, antelope, deer, and elk roam. She and her husband love to travel as well. Her favorite times are spending Christmas Eve with her family and watching her grandsons frolic in the joy of the season.

She has self-published several novels, one children's book, and a non-fiction book that are available on Kindle and Amazon.

The author's last name is pronounced "care." She hopes that's what everyone will do. Care about each other.

Also By C.S. Kjar

Finding Love in the Snow

The people at the Spruce Canyon Lodge make an appearance in *Finding Love in the Snow*. Find out what happens when a young woman is rescued from an avalanche and taken to the lodge.

The Five Grannies Go to the Ball

A children's book with coloring pages, *The Five Grannies Go to the Ball* is about young and old people learning from each other. Having fun has no age limits.

The Sisters of Time Series

Estranged for fifteen years, the three daughters of Father Time must reunite to protect their mother's estate. Old feuds, greedy realtors, ghosts, storms, and sandy beaches provide an enchanting tale of sisters reconnecting.

These and other C.S. Kjar books may be found on her website at **https://cskjar.com/books/**

Visit my website at

http://www.cskjar.com

and my Facebook page at **http://www.facebook.com/cskjar**. You can also follow me on other social media platforms.

Sign up for my newsletter at https://cskjar.com and get a free short story about older women discovering their powers.

AFTERWORD

One of the best things you can do for an author is write a review. Please tell me what you thought of this novel by leaving a review with one or more of your favorite retailers. Even a short review, one or two lines, can be a tremendous help to me. Your review is also a gift to other readers who may be searching for just this sort of story, and they will be grateful that you helped them find it.

If you write a review, please send me an email at cskjar.books@gmail.com so I can thank you with a personal reply. Also, let me know when you tell your friends, readers' groups, and discussion boards about this book.

Thank you very much for your support. C.S. Kjar

Made in the USA
Columbia, SC
11 July 2024

38262216R00083